A Body is a Body

Alexa Faulks

A Body is a Body

JARGON

Jargon

www.jargonbooks.net

This book is a work of fiction. Any references to historical events, real people or real places are used fictitiously.

A Body is a Body

Chapter One: Devon

Devon

I

See, I want to start from the beginning to gain perspective on what I'm about to do. Right now I'm glowing like a hero but I'm sure, after, they will consider me a monster.

"Where's the light? I can't find the light," Blue said, only it was more like he was whining. We were playing the ghost-in-the-mirror game and we'd just flicked the switch. I looked into the darkness for his face but of course I couldn't see it. I couldn't see anything. It was hot and the air wasn't moving around in my small bathroom- unfortunately for the oft drug-sick inhabitants of this cheery little household, the air was always stagnant. Before we turned the lights off we tried to get comfortable as we could. Blue had squeezed next to the toilet and my back was pushing into the towel rack. I was nearest the light switch. Angel got the best spot to the left of the mirror and Cin was right there in the middle, right in front of the mirror. If Maria came she was going to get him first.

Maria had brought us all together. Maria's death. It wasn't that she was so near and dear to us all but that she was so close geographically. We all lived in the same apartment complex. She was a little older than us but not more than a few years. Of course a few years to a kid is like an eternity. Anyway, she'd been shot to death, right there on her boyfriend's couch. It was an accident, in a way, but then it wasn't, too. Like most things. She'd been staying over at her boyfriend's place, a guy who was known to slouch off on his debts in our little society here. Someone got sick of it. This someone pushed into her boyfriend's place with a pistol and started squeezing the trigger. It was Maria's bad luck to have been cozied up next to her boyfriend while they were watching The Jerry Wringer Show. Boom. A shot right to the heart. Five other shots sorted themselves out in the walls and furniture around them but it was

6

only the one that mattered for Maria.

Then it was my mother and my good luck to have been next in line to move from our one-bedroom to Maria's boyfriend's newly vacated two-bedroom apartment. That's why the four of us, Angel, Blue, Cin and myself, found ourselves squeezed into my bathroom that day for a little scary fun.

So, Blue'd been asking about the light. He was nervous, more than a little, about the whole thing. "The light's inside of you, man," Cin said, trying to calm Blue down. Right then I figured Cin was one of those Jesus kids. I could just tell by the way he said it. But we could all sense Blue's fear. It was creeping into our very bones like ice. I heard Angel take a deep breath, like she was going to say something big.

"I can see everything I want to see. Can you guys all just shut up so we can start this thing?" Angel's voice in the air was like a kingdom. The three of us guys just crawled right into it, ready to do as she ruled. "We all have to say it together. On the count of four... One.... Two.... Three.... Four," she said, then all of us said it together:

"Maria, Maria, show us your ghost." We chanted this four times, as we'd planned. One for each of us. Then we were all silent for a while, the excitement and dread in each of us wilting like daisies in every passing second that Maria didn't show. We listened and didn't listen to each other's breathing, we focused on the mirror, on our own thoughts, our close bodies, waiting.

"I think I see it! I see her!" Cin whispered. I was pretty sure we all held our breath and stared into the mirror. Something was there. I swear it. Something bright and small and getting bigger as it came closer. I found the wall with my fingers and felt it up, finding the switch. I held my hand there. The thing was getting too close.

"Oh my god. I knew it. God damn, I knew it," Angel said, her voice excited.

Devon

"Here it is. Finally," Cin whispered. I was a little nervous but I didn't say anything, just held the switch safely in my fingers.

"Is she gone yet? I don't want to see her." Blue's voice was afraid. We all knew he was closing his eyes then. "Please turn on the light. Please. I don't want to see." So I did it. For Blue. I flicked on the light. They all blinked the brightness into view and looked at me.

"Devon, you ruined it," Angel said. Cin looked around and smiled, nodding his head.

"Naw. We all saw it, didn't we? Did you see her face?"

"It had a face?" Blue asked, shaking.

"Good thing I turned on the light. Blue would've had a heart attack," I said, sounding tough. Blue moved to open the bathroom door. "No. If you open the door too soon, you can let the spirit out. And I think she was mad," I said, thinking about how close it was in there, about how I liked it. I looked at my watch. "They say if you wait for thirteen minutes before you open the door then you're safe."

"Who's 'they?'" Angel said. I just looked at her.

"Where's she now then?" Blue asked.

See, the beautiful things won't be still for you without force, or without your having to fool them into it. I knew that back then when we were kids in that bathroom, I know that now. I knock my knuckles on the tabletop, annoyed with myself. I've been trying to stop from remembering certain things. A man is not made up of his past but of his potential in the future. The more I can forget, the more whole I can become; the more my present can begin reflecting my future and my future can act as itself, not a pathetic mixture of past and present and future.

So far, the present, too, is stupid to me. In most cases it's just a sick mass of memories and hope. A contradiction of it's own existence. No one ever lives in the present. They are always hoping or dreaming or remembering. Because of this, the present focuses too much on emotion. And I'm starting to think that emotions are just instincts dolled up in the human intellect. We give them too much credit, analyzing them, as if we were going to find the meaning of life in them. But emotions are all just reflections of our instincts. To try to puzzle-out an emotion is to play a petty mind game with myself. It's to pretend that I'm something more complex than the instincts I and everyone else's been born with, which I don't believe. I hear a knock on the door. The one I've been waiting for.

II

Dr. Ben Sunshine slides the white paper bag across the table. It contains a 100-milligram vial of Succinylcholine. His hand rests on it for a moment and he looks at me, his face a mask of sensibility and control. Suddenly it cracks into a smile.

"Don't tell me what you're going to use it for," he says, winking and smiling at me. Then he lowers his voice though I've taken every precaution to make sure we'd be completely alone in my apartment. "The nurse let me use it on her once. It was like she was dead. I'm telling you, man, it's a whole different thing! She couldn't move a muscle!"

What the good doctor has lifted for me, for more than a small fee, let me tell you, is a paralytic agent. Normally they use it to install a respirator hose down a patient's throat. Without it, the teeth'll clamp shut and the throat muscles'll contract so it's impossible to get the hose down there. They usually give the patient something to knock him out too because it would be torture to go through the procedure. Succinylcholine doesn't paralyze the senses. The patient would remain conscious and the acuity of his senses would probably be heightened because of the potency of the experience. I tell the doc I don't want my "patient" to be unconscious. "Yeah, man. It's better if she feels it, right?" He licks his lips. He does that a lot.

I also don't tell him what other tools I'll need except for

9

the medical book. He'll throw that in for free, he says. I tell him I want to learn about the female organs, about the uterus and the clit. He likes it when I say clit, I can tell. Anyway, the book has everything in it and gives directions on how to perform certain procedures, procedures I can't ask the doc about. It's safer letting him think I'm a necro freak. Like we have something in common. If he knew my real plans for the stuff he'd probably ball out on me. I can't have that.

I met the doc through a friend of my girlfriend's. Real cute girl but dumb as hell. Another quirk Dr. Sunshine and I didn't share. I don't care for them that young. Jenna's my girl, though. She said he'd never touched her. She's a special piece of pie, Jenna. Familiar, tastes like home. We met at the Everett Mall one Saturday and realized we live in the same complex. The Jungle, we call it, right behind the mall. If you want to be sweet you can call it "Green Meadows Housing." She'd moved in several months before. Don't know how I missed her. She was wearing a tiny red dress that day and a smile that shot straight through my gut. I knew right away. The first thing she said to me was crazy. She kept looking back at me following her and then all of a sudden she turns around and waits for me to catch up, checking me out the whole time. I was wearing my hottest blue shirt so I knew she approved.

"So how many times you been in love?" she asks. Can you imagine? What kind of first line is that? I didn't know what to say at first and I just looked at her like an idiot for a few seconds. Then, like a psychopath I say:

"What do you mean, like you want to cut your balls off if you lose it sort of love or the kind that just makes your dick hard?" I don't know where that came from but I said it and as soon as I did I broke up inside. Wrong thing to say, I'm thinking to myself. But Jenna, being who she is, loved it. She smiled like it had been the perfect thing. Our eyes have been locked almost

10

every second since. My dick's been hard almost as often, too. I
think this thing they call love is both though, a hard cock *and*
some vulnerable balls. We've been together now about three
months and she's amazing. I'm going to miss her when I leave.

So, it had really got to me when they messed her up like
that. 26 stitches! *And* an abortion. She's so small, too, only 98
pounds of honey. They didn't have to knock her around like that.
They being Angel, Cinnamon Jim and Blue. Blue.

Jenna's child-sized head had been thumped against the
stall wall when they kicked the door in. Surprised, she fell back
and landed ass-down in the public-dirty toilet bowl, the same one,
just seconds before, she had been so careful not to touch her clean
little thighs to: she's a squatter. This all happened in our upscale
"cabana." It was so snazzy that nobody that had any sense ever
used the toilet in there unless they had no place else in the world
to go. It's where the crackheads are always floating around. I
actually set up shop there once in a while. No matter how much
they do it, they always want more. Its like a never-ending sewer
of money and strange favors. Nasty fuckers They'll do anything
for the shit. But Jenna just couldn't wait until she got to the
apartment even though it was just a few steps away. Said it was
urgent, said she knew those guys were in there but didn't think
they'd bother her. Stupid, because it's not the first time
something like this happened in that same bathroom. And she
knew it. Anyway, Blue took her by the hair and threw her
forward. She slid face down, across the dirty tiled floor, until her
nose met up with Cinnamon Jim's knock off T-Bone boot. He
nudged her face with it a little but then she felt herself being
pulled back. Her skirt was flipped up and she could feel Blue
looking at the pink panties with purple hearts she had chosen
special that morning; they were almost a perfect match with the
purple bra I got her at *Anna's Boutique*. Anyhow, they were
snatched off, she heard them rip and the elastic screamed into her
hips before finally giving up. She wasn't so scared, I mean, of

course she was a little freaked, she was about to be raped, but she knew the guys and, well, to be honest, it's not like she'd never had double pen before- not that that's what she got exactly, but what she thought she'd get, she said. What really scared her was the blood. Little flecks of red started to mix with the mud or shit or whatever was on the tiled floor that her pretty little cheek was pressed into. She wasn't sure where it was coming from but knew that it was probably hers. She looked behind her and saw more blood under Blue's knees, which were now on the floor. What was bleeding? Her head had been knocked, she remembered, but she couldn't feel it because it was numb. Blue pushed in and was more violent than was necessary, she thought. He could've spit on his hand or something. A little lube never hurt anybody. She was able to raise her eyes and see Cinnamon Jim's face.

Cinnamon Jim is the freckled kid. We used to hang out when we were younger. Steal bikes and shit. Looks like somebody sprinkled a God-sized pinch of Cinnamon on his face. He came home from camp one year, like ten years ago, and there they were. Wow! He also came back with an accent. His speech was now clipped with a sort of forced, awkward slang. He drank a lot of Old E 40 ouncers, called them "fowties" and accompanied the name always, with a little sign language. He would press his two middle fingers and thumb together and the remaining pinky and pointer fingers shot out straight back and away form the other three, as if too good for them. He would punch the air with this hand sign- "fowtie. Got to git me a fowtie." Bam. Bam. Since these changes in Cin both came at once, the freckles and the attitude, it gave the impression that he was trying to balance the innocent effect of his freckles on his appearance. He looked more childish but acted tougher.

"Do you have to be so rough, man?" Cinnamon started pacing, his voice was high-pitched. His facial expressions were split: one second he was afraid, then excited but very, very sorry.

Then, of course, horny as hell. He jumped a little, laughed, swore. His hand sometimes shooting out when he wasn't saying anything at all.

"Calm down, man. You ain't got to hurt her. She's doing it anyway…hey man. It's my turn…. C'mon, at least let me get in her ass." Blue let up and moved so Cin could get in her. Blue's pants were bloody where they had touched the floor. Cin pushed in, much smaller than Blue. Gentler too, and there wasn't as much friction since Blue had already broke her in.

When they were done (they had gone crazy. When she came home she had cum on her shirt, her shoes) she stumbled out of the bathroom. There was someone out there who had been leaning against the door. Hey. She knew Angel. Had she been keeping watch?

If there is a leader of their little group, it's Angel. Being the only female and more than slightly attractive she generally makes the major decisions and has usually been able to persuade the guys to do or get whatever she wants. Clothes, some guy's ass kicked, bubblegum. They gave her this name as a joke. First they used it here and there to tease her. She liked bragging to people how she would screw and leave her boyfriends- well, most of them- have them fall for her then bail out. "What an Angel," everybody'd say. And it stuck. She's always chewing watermelon blocks of gum and so when she speaks her words sound gooey and babyish, even though what she actually says might get you to thinking she has a forked tongue. This is part of her charm, some would say. It makes a guy want to eat her, devour her mouths, make her hush. Probably why Blue's so weak over her. She could be Hawaiian. Her pussy smells like the sea. I know this because I fucked her.

Angel moved to the side and her eyes got huge when they saw Jenna.

"What the fuck? What's all that blood, girl? Blue! Cin! Get the fuck out here!" She spit her gum out and tried to help

Jenna stand up. The guys came tumbling out, Blue looking like a wolf, dark and hungry, Cin like a hyena, scared and goofy and greedy. "What did you do to her? You idiots, what if she dies?" Angel hit the two guys on the back of their necks with her free hand. They almost seemed to bend over into them. Plap! Plap! "Take her home."

"What?" the guys said together, almost like it was planned.

"Drop her on her doorstep or something. You can't just leave her like this. Look, just carry her to the edge of the lot over there and I'll pull my car as close as possible." Blue made a growling sound. He hoisted Jenna up, his shoulder pressing suddenly into her gut. She vomited all down his back. He dropped her on reflex and she passed out. When she woke up she was in the hospital. At least they'd done that for her. I'm sure it wasn't Blue who called the ambulance for her though. Not his style. He probably would've let her die in the bathroom. Not out of malice but out of an eerie indifference.

When Blue and I started hanging out, our moms started to know each other. Then they started getting high together. His mom hit it a little too hard once. They used to lock us in one of the bedrooms and leave chips and candy in there so we wouldn't be too pissed. We'd have our own mini-high with all the sugar. They must've been trying to prepare us for the real stuff. Sometimes we could hear them over the music. Anyway, his aunt adopted him after his mom died; she came and moved into her old room. She was weird. He never talked about her though and he wouldn't ask me over either. Once I looked in through the cracked curtain in his bedroom window and saw a big hump under the covers on his bed. His aunt poked her head out suddenly like she sensed me watching and gave me this freaky look. I saw Blue's head, small compared to her bigness, peeping out, no expression, from under her. We never said anything about that. She died recently. He took over the place in the Jungle and he lives there alone now.

When Blue looks at me I get the creeps, even now after I've know him for so long. He's all hooded and I can't tell, still, if he's slightly insane or extremely intelligent. His eyes are full of secrets and a crazy blue color. That's why he's called Blue. He's tall and slim, solid, which is why women love him. Men too. When he's nervous he talks. Mostly about bullshit. He does it with anyone who tries to get close to him, even me. He'll be loud as if he were trying to talk over some aspect of himself he didn't want me to see, like he was trying to distract me from seeing something, talking so I wouldn't notice. It worked for the most part, too. I still don't know the monster. I do know he has a huge dick. I know this because I fucked him too. If anyone's wondering it's called being secure in your sexuality. A body is a body. A hole is a hole. A heart is a heart. And I ain't nothing but a man.

I feel a little like a woman now, though, having to learn this sewing business. Jenna's got them on her head, the stitches, so when I practice, after I'm done, I can even compare my stitches to hers to see if they look right. The medical book is working out to be very handy. It teaches you how to do anything you can possibly think of.

Blue and I have been going back and forth with each other's girlfriends for a while. It started with Angel. She was Blue's girl at one point, the one he liked a lot actually, but she started feeling for me. Now, me and Blue were friends but he always gets the nice girls and I really couldn't help it if Angel was into me. I mean, I couldn't change the girl's feelings. She's so sexy too. Round little ass, thin arms. So, things happened and he found us in his bed. Of course he went crazy, which is why I have a five-inch slash scar decorating my upper left arm. He went over to my house after that and got up in my girl, who, no matter what he said, was thinking of me the whole time. It's been two years since then and we've both had a few different girlfriends. Cinnamon Jim thinks it's funny to say that the only reason some of my girls get with me is because they know Blue's going to come after them. I bet that's why most of Blue's girls get with him, because they know how I'm in the picture. Yes, some may be more interested in our rivalry than our compassionate personalities. Angel and him didn't talk for a while after but then started hanging suddenly as friends, I guess. She barely looks at me now when we pass each other, not that I want her to. I already got her in every hole she's got and she loved it. Arched her back like a little cat for me. Spread her woman's legs. Chewed her watermelon gum.

But it's all gone too far now. This little campfire we had going is out of control. Jenna was hurt bad. What made Blue get so violent? And why the hell did he have to bring Cin and Angel into it? Now Jenna's saying she wants to go to Blue herself, that she has something to tell him that she can't tell me. But I know she's still a little dizzy from the rape. She's talking crazy talk. Some people just need someone else to speak up for them. Some people are weak.

I've got to show her that Blue can and will be fixed for what he did to her. I'll settle things. This is where the medicine comes in. Succinylcholine. It'll heal things alright, kill the sickness that exists between Blue and I. I'll never have to worry about him again. I have it all figured out now but I have to be careful because he'll be expecting something.

The guy's alone as much as people will let him be. It shouldn't be that hard to get him set up for the procedure. When we used to hang together it was always because I forced him to come out, to get up off his soggy couch and play pool or something. He was always moping around, watching bad TV. Not cable, he couldn't afford it, but TV, crumby sit-coms and whatnot. I used to ask him why he likes seeing other people live their lives but doesn't like living his own. He never did answer me. He would raise his scarred up wrists whenever he didn't

16

want to answer a question. Once, he did it real slow, without even turning his face away from the screen, like he was reminding me he didn't care about anything, not his life, the world and especially not my question. He tried it twice, so far as I know, suicide. I saved him one of those times. He had known I was coming over before he started though so I don't know if I really saved him since he knew he wasn't really going to die. He knew I'd stop him when I got there.

I decided to plan it for 1:30 AM on Monday morning. He was sure to be home alone then, Monday being a no-pussy-getting day, as we used to joke, and him without a girlfriend.

III

I've been watching his place from the bushes since midnight on, saw him stumble in from the dive at around 12:30, saw the lights turn on then off again. I saw him through his bedroom window. He lives on the bottom floor. I know exactly how to get to his room- he's kept the same one since forever. My stuff's all packed in the car. Said bye to Mama as best I could. Gave her the rest of my stash, anyway. She'll probably kick it soon, she's so skinny. See ya, Mama.

I am checking and rechecking my materials, knowing I can't mess this up or the guy will be dead and I know I can't bear that on my conscience. I mean, I hate Blue and am tired of the whole game but we grew up together,. He's practically blood. No matter how bad Jenna was hurt I can't forget how Blue and I used to go shoot BBs at the neighbors' windows together, race each other through the lot to the mall.

I am opening the bag (also supplied free from our good Dr. Sunshine) and running my fingers over the materials. The vial of the paralytic agent contains exactly 100 milligrams. The doctor told me any more than that without a pro around to keep track could make things permanent. This amount would only

17

have him paralyzed for seven minutes tops so I'll have to work fast. The syringe is here with its plastic cap. All I have to do is take off the cap and push the needle into the vial, which was specially made for the thing, and then pull the inner tube back. Just like a normal needle. Like mom has. Then take it out after all the stuff is sucked in there and point it up so any air bubbles surface and I can ("gently") tap the tube and push it up a little to get them out. Dr. Sunshine reminded me that I didn't want to get any air into him, him Blue, or it could be deadly. He said I have to get as close to a vein as possible. The closer to his bloodstream I get it the sooner he'll go down and the longer, also, that he'll stay down. I know he'll probably wake up the second I get the needle into him so wherever I hit first will have to do.

It'll be easy to find his vein, though; I'm kind of a pro at that. When I was younger my mom used to get me to shoot her up in the places she couldn't reach, like the back of her leg. Real heavy addicts' veins dry up after they use them so much so she ran out of places she could reach, where the veins were usable. I remember being kind of relieved I didn't have to be locked up in the room. After I helped her I could stay in the living room and watch TV. Scooby Doo, here I come. The veins in the back of the leg are not so easy to spot so she'd take this big rubber band and get it up around her thigh. The veins'd surface after awhile and I could feel them with my fingers. I'll tell you, though, it's the worst thing in the world to see your mom in her panties when you're that age. When you're any age. Blue always made fun of me for that.

Whenever I look at the scalpel next to that needle I get chills. I can't really sort out whether they're excited chills or scared-out-of-my-mind chills. It's all coming from the same place, I guess. Then there's the twisty chords to tie the matter up, the tiny scissors I'll use to cut the chords, the gauze and the tape I need to patch him up, the flashlight, the stitching thread and needle. I really got the sewing thing down, being the good little

A Body is a Body

housewife I am. Got the numbing serum that I lifted from my
dentist a few months back with its needle that I can just push into
him wherever. Don't need to find the vein. Funny. Thought I'd
be using it for something totally different. I brought the med
book just in case my mind blanks. Got the tickets I'll be needing
to get my ass out of town. There's the cock block, as a call it. I
have to be right on about this. I'll have to make sure the bandage
is tight so he won't bleed out. Then there's the breather. Because
he'll probably stop breathing when he becomes paralyzed, I need
to put the breather to his mouth and pump it every minute or so,
so he won't suffocate. At 1:30 AM Blue should be in a deep
enough stupor so that I probably won't wake him when I come in.
I bet he passed out the second he fell onto his army cot of a bed.
Poor bastard.

   It's 1:28 AM and my stomach's gone sour. My hands are
sweating and I'm hot, so hot. I think I'm in a fever. It can wait.
It has to. I have the bag over my shoulder and I'm going in. The
door's unlocked just like he's always left it since we were kids
("if they wanna get in they'll get in. I don't want 'em breaking
my door to do it"). It squeaks, of course. I'm closing it behind
me and the place reeks. I don't know if I can handle it. It smells
like body and semen and piss. There's hardly any air. I press on
the flashlight. Jesus. What is that shit in the corner? Don't look
at it. OK. His room is to the right. Wall. OK. Use the light.
The closer I'm getting to his room the stronger the smell's
getting. He can't have had a girlfriend for a while. She wouldn't
put up with this. I can't help it, I have to vomit.... There. A little
better. I'm sure he can't hear me. My watch glows 1:32 AM.
I'm in the room now. I'm trying to breath without making any
noise. I open the bag and finger the different things in its
compartments. Did I get the twisties? Yes. Syringe, vial. Fuck.
Are his eyes open? No. He'll be used to the dark since he's been
laying in it. He'll be able to see me even if I can't see him
because I'm not used to the blackness yet. Fuck. They are open.

Devon

No.

     Cap off. Syringe in vial. Pull inner tube. Bubbles surface. I have to see them with the light though. Tap "gently," push. A tiny squirt of the stuff comes out and I kneel on the floor next to the bed, next to Blue's face. I can see a little now. Jesus. I touch his arm. *Wake up goddamit. Stop me.* His eyes are closed. I feel the vein. Just like Mama's are. A soft little rope. Push the needle in. He tenses. His eyes are open. Jesus. Those eyes. I feel them even in the dark. He moves a little and looks surprised like I don't remember seeing him look before. Now I have the scalpel ready in my hand so he sees it. He's looking at it from the side of his eyes, breathing, wondering. Doctor said it takes about three minutes to take full effect. He's weak already though. I must've got it right in the vein. Now he's trying to grab me but he can't get a grip. He's saying something but it sounds like his mouth is full of glue. He's still now. Timer on. OK. Work quickly. Turn on the light. Shut the blinds. Set the breather. I pull down the sheet and see that he still sleeps naked. His skin seems to lick my fingers. I push his legs apart. pump the breather. Thank God his eyes are closed. I tape his penis down on his stomach. It's soft and hard at the same time. Is that some effect of the drug? I prop his balls on the block. He doesn't move. I shoot the numbing stuff into that place between his asshole and his sack and then in his sack too, just to be safe. I want him knowing what's going on but he'd probably fall unconscious if he could actually feel it. His sack's like butter when I press the scalpel through. It's been about 45 seconds.

     "Blue, I know you can hear me and are probably going crazy right now. You can't move. Can't breathe." I pump the breather. The sack opens easily and his wet jewels fall into my hand, still attached. "We can't keep doing this to each other. You can't keep doing this to me. And you won't." They feel like skinned grapes and are about the size of walnuts. There is not much blood yet, just as the book said. "I'm leaving once we're done here and you'll never see me again." My tears are just extra, I don't know where they're coming from but they're blurring my view a little. I use the tiny scissors to snip and snip the kiddy beads from his body. I put them in my pinch-and-seal baggie and place them in a compartment in the bag. More blood now. The twisties. They'll dissolve after a couple weeks. I am hurrying to tie up his useless chords. The blood flow is curbed almost immediately. "This'll probably make you dull. You hear me? I'm taking all your hormones away here, I'm taking your children. No more loving for you. I am so, so sorry, though. I wish you hadn't made me do this. Stay away from Jenna now, from all my women. Just leave them alone. Do you hear me?" I am sewing up the split sack now. It's been about five minutes. I put some disinfectant on him and leave it on the floor with some fresh bandages for when he wakes up. An infection could kill him. I wrap him up and tape him badly but it works. Everything goes back in the bag. I'll just have one more kiss. His lips are so soft.

  His eyes open. I almost fall back. He still doesn't move. His eyes are just watching me. Can I fix it? "What'd I do? God! I'm so sorry Blue." I run out of the apartment and to my car. I'm at the airport in two hours. Usually it takes three.

IV

  When I got to the place I'd reserved in Fort Walton Beach, Florida, which is old and crooked but very private, I put Blue's jewels out to dry on the back deck. At first I was afraid somebody might see them but then what if they did? They'd never guess it. Probably think they were fish eyes. They dried up nice after stinking up the place for a few days. Got smaller and almost weightless. I bought a special glass box for them that I keep in the back of my closet, locked. The balls hold the majority of a guy's sex hormones and hormones control the emotions. Guess that means I took Blue's ability to feel love? Even to feel.

21

Devon

He's probably thanking me for it, being all depressed like he was. Maybe this calmed him down. His sickness was a result of his loving, really. But he's stupid to give his instincts so much credit, personalizing them, making emotions out of them until he's screwed into thinking it's all about his character. That kind of thinking could kill a man.

Chapter Two: **Blue**

A Body is a Body

I

I kicked the pile of the sweets after they shut the door, good and hard, hoping she'd hear me. She didn't, or pretended she didn't, anyway. Devon stomped a candy bar right in half. Guess nobody'll be eating that one. Not even her. There are a few bags of chips in the corner and cola on the bed. Enough for the both of us, plus. I hate how there's no TV in here. There's not even a window. Just Devon, me and our ears. We have books, though. Old stuff from the library that shut down. But we can hear everything and they think we can't. They moan every once in a while. And there are men that come, none that we know besides from their scratchy, loud voices. Sometimes he and I try to talk over them but it seems so obvious and impossible so we usually just end up sitting there quiet, reading or coloring or whatever, eating our sweets and listening.

"I'm sick of this. I want to run away. She's not being a mom," I say through my teeth. I'm trying not to pout but it's hard.

"Fuck those bitches, Blue. They're doing drugs in there, you know, that's what those needles are for." He's quiet and looks at my face for a second, to see if this surprises me but it doesn't, of course. His eyes are really brown, almost black. They always look excited but then also sad, like he's been promised too many things in life that almost, but never quite, came through. I'm careful not to make any expression. I just look at him until he looks away like he always does. Then he goes: "You know what to do? Just ignore her, act like she's not a real person. They're not, you know. They're zombies. They're dead like zombies." His mouth is full of gumdrops and little flecks of sweet spit come from his mouth and land on my cheek and upper lip. He starts looking, angry, past my head at the wall as if he's imagining their zombie bodies there. His hands start motioning their height and weight and I suddenly feel like I hate him.

"Stop. You're spiting on my face. Not all the time,

though. She's not always like that. At least MY mom isn't. She's nice sometimes too. Not when she's like this, but sometimes. After it's over." Devon gets up and starts walking around the room with his arms straight out in front of him, hands dangling from the wrists. His chubby face is dead-like, eyelids droopy, and he's making stupid monster moaning noises.

"Oooh! Oh! I'm going to sit on you! With my fat mama ass!"

"Shut up, Devon. It's not funny. My mom's not that fat. Just because yours is all bones doesn't mean—"

"—But it's not fair. Mom's aren't s'posed to be like this, they're s'posed to take care of us and feed us right—"Devon starts, getting cut off by some weird sound. He takes off his shoe and throws it at the door before either of us figure out what he's doing. "You zombies! You shit zombies!" he screams, and at the same time widens his eyes. He can't believe he yelled it like that. Neither can I. Everything is suddenly quiet. We make a run for the bed and dive under it. Safe.

"Nurse! Nurse! It's happening! Give me something! Nurse!" Some flash of white dashes in with a needle.

"No need to scream, dear. Here you go... sh sh shhhh. You're OK now. Shhhh." The stuff she puts in my arm warms me, cell by cell, and I lean back on my pillow. I can see her, just barely, looking over me, stretching her mouth into a chubby and obscene grin. She begins rubbing my thigh, slow and hesitant at first, kind of testing me to see if I'll knock her hand away. "Yes. You're alright now, aren't you?" I don't care enough to push her hand. My body feels too calm all of a sudden. "Oh, my! You certainly did have your meds today, didn't you! You're a very BIG boy today," she giggles.

A Body is a Body

II

I'm thinking about how I'm not tied to the bed and about how I feel violent and that I should be, I should be tied to the bed. I smile, knowing that they don't know, they couldn't know, because I've hidden it well and am a master at hiding things. I don't have any sharps but my two hands can do a lot, I think. They are strong and the nails have grown just a teensy bit since they cut them, enough so that maybe I could do a little damage to this incomplete body I've got. Just one little break and I'm free. Just one little break in the skin and I'm free.

The walls are all white, so are the sheets and so is the goddam pillow. There's a tiny peephole of a window that looks out into the white hallway where the nurses shuffle by, poking their greedy little eyeballs through every hour to get a look at the freak with hardly any fingernails. I'm going to have to talk to somebody about that. A guy needs his fingernails. A guy needs to scratch every here and there. I pull back the gauze on my wrists carefully and am thinking about trying to reopen one of the wounds there and in walks Angel.

I straighten the bandages quickly without her seeing. She talks to the nurse for a second in a quiet voice and then turns towards me. A surprise in a purple top, almost as delicious as the morphine. The nurses didn't tell me she was coming. The thread-thin arms of her nighttime hair reach to the middle of her back, fondling her shoulders, her upper waist. She sits next to me and I can't help but put my face in her hair when she turns to hug me. It smells so warm. She's all smiles, which is strange for her. She's sorry for me. Teeth like beautiful little pearls. She's not chewing her gum today, either, and I kind of miss how her jaw pumps and flexes while she wrestles it around in her mouth. It seems wrong that she doesn't have it. But I bet security took it from her. She is looking around the room, painted so terribly in white, and asks if I want some photos to put up.

"It's so white. Can't they give you a blanket with some

fucking color in it? What is this shit? They're trying to make you go nuts is what they're doing," she says. I watch her lips. They're as suckable as plums.

"Technically I am nuts. I guess they figure they can't make it any worse. I can't stand white though."

"Gives me the creeps. Maybe white sheets're cheaper. Maybe they get them in bulk or some shit." Now there seems like nothing to say and nothing to look at. Her eyes flit between the bleached corners of the room, trying to find a perch. I listen to her breathing. I want to put my hand on hers like it's supposed to be but I know she'd push it away. She bounces the rubber heel of her shoe on the floor and begins studying her hand, holding it out in front of her like a menu. Her nails are Barbie-doll pink and the polish is a little chipped. The blood runs beneath the skin of her hand in greenish, merging rivers. The bed moans when she gets up. I sit and watch her, her hair moving with the sway of her body. She begins sliding her finger along the wall as she edges around the room. The pink fingernail shouts against the white. She walks towards the wall opposite so I watch her ass, small and compact, the muscles driven and able beneath her taught skin, her jeans.

"So you did it again, huh?" she says, looking at the bandages on my wrists. Her voice is cold and I shiver. I think of pretending that I don't know what she's talking about but I know it'll be a waste of our thirty minutes. "I just don't get it. Why'd you guys have to mess the bitch up like that? None of this would've happened."

"Of course I did it again, Angel. You understand what he did to me, right?" I ask, my voice polluting her space. She's quiet and has paused. Her finger is still and quiet on the wall. She breathes and her chest moves and all I want to do is be silent and part of her air. I want to tell her I'm sorry but I have no reason to and I hate myself for it.

"It must've been those meds they pumped into you. You

27

weren't thinking about all that suicide shit when you weren't getting those. You do look more like yourself now, though." Her eyes rush over my body. I try to straighten up, stop slouching but it's too late, she's already looking away. "Does it hurt now? Did it hurt when he did it? You never really talked about it," she says, not looking at me. Her voice is the only live thing in the room.

"He numbed me. I couldn't feel it. I can't feel it now, either. It's all healed. Besides, I get so many painkillers that I can't even feel my legs." The walls suck up the sounds we make like hungry wolves whose silence seems to howl back at us, searching and racing and seething. She turns to look at me from the side of her eye. She usually doesn't look me full in the face for more than a second.

"Cin said you were conscious when Devon did it."

"Yeah." Pause.

"Shit. I'm so sorry, Blue. How do you bear it?" I smile inside, wondering about the time, about my next shot.

"I try not to think about it. I keep getting these crazy flashbacks, though. The meds help but they're just a cover up. It's like being on fire and then being given a glass of water. No matter how good it tastes, it can't make you forget you're on fire."

"Shit. Can I do something for you? Shit." I say nothing for a moment and just rub my damp fingers together.

"Love me, Angel," I beg, hating the sound of my voice and how it seems to twist her face into a delicately disgusted expression. She closes to me almost instantly and turns away, hard.

"You know I can't make myself love you. Stop messing around." I knew she'd say that. I reload and shoot a lesser bullet:

"Sneak me in a razor, then." She turns and looks at me, quiet, and then starts walking around the room again, sliding her finger slowly. "You don't know how I feel, Angel. I'm in hell. I live in hell. You don't know the memories. The memories alone could kill me anyway. You have no idea."

She says nothing as I watch her, waiting. The silence in the room is starting to make me nervous. I feel like I'm dropping down into something, my vision throbs and I have to put my hand against the wall so I don't fall back onto the bed. This pain. What has he done to me? I want the nurse. Just now, the nurse knocks on the window, her demonic eyes peeping in with their 'it's time' look. Angel looks at me and comes over to rustle my hair. I need more than that. I pull at her sleeve and she bends over to hug my skinny self, all full of drugs and sickness.

III

The psychologist looks me right in the eye, which I respect him for because not many people seem to be able to do that. He sits behind the desk, bald, short, and has bushy eyebrows with a deep furrow between, as if he's been frowning in contemplation his whole life. He taps his fingers lightly on the surface of his oak desk and takes a deep breath. I can smell the cinnamon spritz he must've recently used. The room is warm and somehow both stifling and comfortably secure.

"So. Where should we start, Mr. Hoffler?"

"Actually, I'd like it if you called me Blue."

"Blue. Alright. I think I can do that. And how about you call me Albert."

"Good stuff, then, Albert." I sit in my overstuffed chair, resting my skinny arms on its cushy, flora-clad fabric rests and tap my bare left foot. I never wear shoes in this place. They think shoes would be a threat to me somehow, or that I would hide something in the soles. Albert leans back in his springy chair and it creaks, just like they do in the movies.

"So, are you comfortable here at our institution? Are the nurses treating you well, giving you all the meds you need?" I think of telling him the nurses are as perverted as the lowest of the desperate with cocks and no consequences but I don't want anyone messing with my meds. There's no place in the world that's completely safe as it is. This is as good as any, even better because of the meds. At least for now. He probably wouldn't believe me, anyway. They never do. I just nod my head. "Okay, then. How about we start from the time period after it happened."

"After what happened, Albert?"

"I think you know what I'm referring to, Blue. The procedure."

"Ohhh. That time period. Well. I guess I don't mind going into it. As long as it remains between you, me and Dr. Sunshine as was promised."

"Of course, Blue. You have my word. As a psychologist, aside from our particular deal, I am not, by law, allowed to discuss anything I talk about with my patients with anyone other than my patients."

"OK. Here we go, then." I take a deep breath and lean back in my own chair, without the spring action, and let my head drop back. I close my eyes. "Initially, I thought I could just let it heal, not tell anyone about it. I knew I had to keep this to myself if it was in any way possible. It was bound to get around town if I didn't. It's big news, big enough to be talked about in the papers, I imagined, so I didn't tell. Not at first, anyway. Who would want people, anybody, to know that kind of thing?" I say, laughing a little. I open my eyes and pull my head up to look at the psychologist who is calmly watching me, leaning over the desk now with his hand propping up his chin. He nods, listening. "After a few weeks, though, my body started changing in unbearable ways. When he took my balls, Dr. Sunshine said, I lost the majority of my hormonal juices, especially testosterone. Of course that means I lost complete interest in any type of sex acrobatics, as I call them. No amount of porn could get my dick to move an inch." I look at him to see if he is laughing but he isn't. It's not funny when you can't get it up. I guess everybody knows that. I lean my head back again.

Blue

"Go on. Feel comfortable, Blue. I'm here to help you," he says. I am convinced, almost. I hope he can help me. It feels like he can help me. It is eerie having every inch of his attention on me though; I am so open and naked. But it feels good too, it feels like *finally*.

"But even worse was the fact that I began physically changing." I can't help the way my voice has started to shake and it irritates me. I try clearing my throat. "The loss of testosterone made my hips bigger and my shoulders narrower. I even started to lose my chest hair. Not that I ever had much. And my muscles got as soft as Angel's"

"Angel?"

"Angel is my ex girlfriend. My friend. She and Cin were good to me but freaked out after it happened. I don't think they knew how to treat me anymore. Angel wanted to call an ambulance when she found me a couple days later. I'm lucky she came when she did because the bandages Devon had left for me were running low and I was hungry. I did convince her to let it be for a while, to let me heal on my own. That was before I started looking womanish, though. But Cin cleaned up and she got me everything I needed and helped me around some. At first I couldn't even get out of bed, you know, either I couldn't or I didn't want to."

"Okay. We'll have to discuss Angel and... Sin? Is that what you called him? Next time we'll see what we can figure out about them," he says, watching me carefully. But he wants to get to the root of the issue now, obviously.

"Maybe. But anyway, besides physical changes I was emotionally dead. It was almost impossible to care about anything. I didn't even mind about Angel anymore, that she didn't love me. At first I was disturbed to madness at what happened but after a week or so I didn't really care. It was weird. But then it wasn't, too. Dr. Sunshine said that's what happens after something like that.

31

A Body is a Body

"Uh huh."

"When Cin and Angel finally convinced me to go in, Sunshine set me up with testosterone shots and told me he'd do everything free if I'd cooperate in a private study. This study, I guess. They promised nobody'd know who I was. No one except the doctor and a psychologist. Right? And you guys are paying for everything, right?" Albert nods his head yes. He folds his hands neatly on the desk and leans towards me, his eyes soft and interested.

"Now. I know this is extremely difficult for you but it will make you feel a thousand times better if you can get it out. That's how you heal. When you talk you are extracting the negativity out of your system, enabling yourself to flush the toilet, so to speak." His eyes light up and I sense excitement brimming beneath his surface. "Otherwise, all the pain and suffering you're experiencing emotionally will putrefy inside of you and, aside from the mental stagnation and melancholy you'd eventually become overwhelmed by, it's likely that the stress from the emotional pain would encourage a series of physical ailments. Do you understand?" His large, rubbery lips glisten with spittle. I notice a perfectly round bead of sweat over his left eyebrow. I nod my head yes. For a moment we sit in silence. His eyes become calm and when they do, my chest tightens up. I know what he is going to ask, what he must ask next. "So. What about the event itself. Were you awake? Did he have you tied up?" I can't make myself respond, my throat is thick. The night it all happened pushes itself into my head, my heart; tears float on the edges of my eyelids. I blink, so they work their way out and onto my cheeks. "Maybe you can nod, yes or no, for me. Were you awake when your testicles were removed?" My throat is heavier than I can bear and suddenly it explodes into a sob. I nod my head yes.

IV

Blue

"Mr. Hoffler, you've got a gift," sings the nurse as she glides into my room without knocking. I turn off my headphones (the Friday "privilege") and duck into my shirt to cover my bare chest.

"It's Blue. Stop calling me Hoffler."

"It's from Angel."

"Yeah?"

"You excited?" She pulls a stuffed bear the size of my head from behind her back and makes it dance in front of my face. "Hello, there! I'm Mr. Bear and I want to hug you!" she says in a baby voice. I grab for it but she snatches it away. "Oh! Is that how you ask for something? By grabbing? You know better than that."

"May I have my bear, please?"

"What'cha gonna give me?" She is smiling and I ask what she wants. She nods her head. "You know…"

"How come no one around here has a goddam husband? This is blackmail. You can't keep doing this to me."

"Doing what? Aren't we giving you all the meds you need? You have a dose scheduled in 15 minutes. Are you ready for it?" I let my head droop to my chest. Just her mention of it makes me swell up inside.

"Yes," I say quietly. They know I'm hooked. They know I can't move without it, can barely breathe. "Could I maybe have a little extra this time?" I ask, my voice a weak whine. The nurse sits down next to me on the bed and hands me the bear.

"I think that might be okay since you're dosing for two now, aren't you," she says, indicating toward the bear. Her voice is hot and intimate. I can smell the garlic she had for lunch. I heave gently. My stomach is very sensitive lately. I take a breath.

"Yes," I say, finally, smiling a little. "I need more this time." Her lips reach like anxious insects for my neck. She pushes me back on my bed and straddles me, the white skirt crawling up and up until I can see the lumpy blue veins in her thighs through her nylons. Her weight makes the bed weep and sag beneath us; I hold my breath as she moves to feel me in her.

V

It is the same bear I gave a Angel for our first anniversary. Does this mean she will love me? It's brown with big eyes, the size of small apricots, and a swirly heart design on the belly. There's a collar around its neck that says 'Andy.' A little boy bear. I lay down with Andy and kiss his hard nose. It smells like her, quietly coconut. I notice a tiny sewed-up tear under his armpit. She must've been rough with it after we broke up. Wait. It's loose. I pull out the thread and the cut opens up. A little stuffing, more thread. Now, something shiny. I pull out a brand new razor blade. 'McNaught's razor,' it reads on the side in brownish lettering. There is also a small square of folded paper: a note.

Blue.

I couldn't make myself say goodbye to you. You know. I hate being sentimental. Devon called from his new spot in Florida and asked me to come down. So I'm going. He feels fucked up for what he did. Of course that's a load of bullshit but you know how I feel about him. I'm sorry. I have to do this for myself. And here is the one real thing I could ever do for you, Blue. –Angel

It is so sharp. I touch it lightly with my thumb and blood comes. Just one little break and it's over. It's been over anyway, since Mama died. And now Angel. She's dead to me now, too. That motherfucker got her. The bare bulb above my head catches the eye of the razor and shoots a light around the room, cutting thin, bright streaks in the walls and ceiling. I angle it so the light slices across my wrist and the fresh scars there. Hmmm….

"Nurse!" She rustles in and I notice she's applied fresh lipstick. The old stuff is in a ring around my dick. "I missed you, Deirdre," I coo, making a motion for her graying blond curls. I caress them. She smiles and I can see the lipstick has made a line across her teeth.

"So soon, you little devil. The extra meds seemed to hit the spot, didn't they?"

"They sure did honey," I say, carefully swinging her around so I can hold her from behind. "They sure did." I swiftly bring my hand up and slit her fat throat, voice box and all. I look into those greedy little eyes that have become so grossly familiar. They seem to not understand, not believe. Blood pumps from the wound steadily. She makes some sucking, gurgling sounds and finally goes limp in my arms. I let her slide, almost quietly, to the floor. My shirt's sopping bloody now so I pull it over my head and throw it to cover her expired face. I bend down, grab her keys and, bare-chested, walk out into the hallway. Now. Which way to the med lab?

Chapter Three:
Cinnamon Jim

A Body is a Body

I

"Why don't you go ahead and git me a fowtie while you're in there," I told her, too sunk down in the sofa to get up and get it myself. Imagine me, Jameson "Cinnamon Jim" Taylor making my mama into my personal butler. All it does is make sense.

"You know you can't have alcohol anymore," she had said, trying to make her voice hard. I hate that voice. I hear it and I get this thickness in my chest. I feel like hitting something. I pushed empty bottles, microwave dinner wrappers and tin-can-made-ashtrays aside and found an old bottle cap on the table. I held it tight for when she came back into the room. The ridges notched into my skin. When she strolled back in with her shirt unbuttoned one too many I could almost see her whole saggy ass tit. It was obvious she wasn't wearing a bra and her nipple was popping out against the dirty-white rayon fabric like a bean, like a nugget of rabbit shit. She was holding her second Jack and Coke of the night in one hand, the glass as tall as my arm is long, and a half-smoked ciggy in the other. I squeezed the bottle cap.

"You got yourself a cozy little drink there, ain'tcha?"

"You mind your business, boy. At least until your daddy gets home. And don't use that tone with me." She sat down and had to unbuckle her belt and undo the top button of her neon green jeans so they didn't cut into her fat. I can say what ever the fuck, in whichever tone I feel the need to. She knows I can and I do. She and Dad are my little bitches now, since I started getting sick. I had thought I should remind her though, since this fact seemed to have been diluted by her whiskey. I got up to face her.

"Dad ain't gonna do shit," I said, not quite as calmly as I'd hoped. I even sounded a little shaky. This is when I snapped the cap at her. It bounced off her cheek and hit the glass. Cracked it. I saw little seeds of liquid sprouting from the sides, growing over her hand. Her cheek got red and I saw a tiny, bright scratch where it had hit. My heart moved real quick in my chest. She looked at me shocked for a few seconds, and then her glass just fell apart. Her drink went all over the front of her, in her lap. She started crying, just in time for Alexa to walk in the front door and see. Excuses bucked through my mind, then. I hate it when Alexa sees me acting like a monster. After the girl dropped her school bag on the floor she even went into the bathroom to get a towel to clean up my mess. But not before she had looked at me with those eyes of hers that see past all my bullshit, and shook her head. Mom, of course, caught my weakness and had started crying harder, not able to stand the guilt that I felt. She could see it in my face.

"Alexa, leave it. You don't need to stand up for me. I'm the mother here. Get that towel away from me."

II

"Mama. Mama!" I don't know why I'm whispering since I am trying to wake her up. It's late though and Alexa's sleeping. Mama snorts a good one, then sighs deep, like she knew her sleep wasn't gonna last.

"Eh? What? What's the matter, honey?"

"Well, nothing, I guess. I just wanted to say sorry."

"Sorry? What? Are you ok?"

"Yeah. I'm fine. Tonight, earlier. I threw the cap. Sorry." I can see her head raised in the dark now and can imagine her sleeping expression, all confused, her mouth falling open.

"Oh, baby, it's alright. I know you just get a little anxious sometimes. I'm sorry too, baby," she says into the darkness. "Want to sleep in here tonight?"

"Alright. Yeah. My head's killing me. I'll sleep in the chair here."

"Is it that bad, Jimmy?"

"It hurts pretty good," I say, feeling the aching as I speak.

"Turn on the light. I'm gonna get up and get your medicine." I can hear her moving and I flick on the light. She blinks, blind for a few seconds. Finally she can see but not without squinting. "Tell me what it feels like." I don't want to say, knowing she'll be upset, but my expression gives me away. "Oh, damn, baby, what did I do? Oh honey, come here," she whines. It sounds like she's going to cry. "Have you been drinking?" She looks at me and I don't answer. Don't need to. "What did I do to my son? Oh God, what did I do?" She holds me and presses her face into my chest.

"It's alright. It's my own fault." I can feel her tears all wet on me.

"How could it possibly be your fault? You're just a baby. A baby." She gets up and takes me into the bathroom, gives me the medicine that hardly ever works anymore. Then we hear Dad stumble in. He seems to be singing Michael Jackson.

"I'm bad! I'm bad! You know it, chm'on." We can hear him stop and do some turns and dips. Probably some finger-points and hip swings. The same ones he always does, I'm sure.

"Jim," Mama calls, "you've got to be more quiet. Jimmy's sick. He's gonna sleep in the room with us tonight." She moves out of the bathroom and flips on the light in the front room.

III

"Cin! Cin!" I can hear the voice through the door I should've shut, from my room. Somebody's got their head poking through the window in there that I also should've shut. "Cin!"

"Shhhh!" Mama and Dad are still sleeping. I get up real slow from the chair and tiptoe out of their room and shut the door.

"Cin!"

"Shhh, motherfucker!" I yell-whisper. "My folks are sleeping. Shhhh!" I get into my room and shut the door, careful not to make it click when the lip of it catches. It's Blue. He looks messed up. "Where're you coming from, man?"

"From Heaven, Cin, where do you think?"

39

Cinnamon Jim

"Didn't they have you in the hospital? You broke out?"

"Oh yeah, I broke the fuck out." I open the window wider and turn on the light. We're both blinking and tearing from the bright. Dark. Light. Dark. Light. Light. I rub my eyes. He hops in and makes himself comfy on my pillow. His ass is on my pillow. His lips are crazy dry and now his eyes are drifting all over the place.

"What's wrong with you, brother? You look fucked up."

"Well. Now that's not a nice thing to say to a favorite friend, now is it?" His speech is a little thick. Suddenly he seems to clear up, though. His eyes focus and he looks at me. I notice his wrists are bandaged. He doesn't have any shoes. He's wearing hospital blues and has a backpack strapped on. I get my slippers and push them on his feet. He puts his hand on my shoulder. "Shit, Cin. You're skinny as fuck. Hasn't your mama been feeding you?" His hand is freezing. I shrug him off.

"What's up, Blue. What do you need? You hungry? You need a place to sleep?" I stand in front of him and put my hands on his shoulders. His eyes, blue as ever, stand out more now because there're dark circles around them, like he never learned how to sleep. His hair is falling in tangled strands around his face, which looks rougher than when I last saw it.

"I need you to get your stuff packed so you can come to Florida with me," he crackles. His voice sounds broken.

"How are you getting to Florida? And why Florida?"

"We're taking your car. And we're going to Florida because that motherfucker is there."

"Devon?" I feel my stomach drop.

"Yeah."

"How do you know?"

He pulls out a small square of crumpled paper and pushes it into my hand. He lets his head drop to his chest so I can't see his eyes. I straighten the paper out and read, trying to feel prepared. He's quiet.

A Body is a Body

"...'and here is the one real thing I could ever do for you'? What does she mean by that?"

"She sent me a razor blade with it," he says, looking up at me with a smile. I shiver a little.

"A razor? What? That fucking whore. How could she—"

"I asked her to. Don't worry about it. Our point is that he's in Florida." Blue looks at me very seriously, very still. "I can get their exact whereabouts from Angel's mom. I'll make a call tomorrow. So we'll go, alright? Alright, Cin?" His eyes beg me.

"Can we leave in the morning?" I say, thinking of saying goodbye to Mama. He pauses and watches my eyes, then he says:

"Naw. It's got to be tonight. I may have hustled up a little trouble at the hospital." He watches me closely.

"What'd you do, Blue?" My mind flickers over the possibilities. I cringe.

"Oh, you know. A little razzle-dazzle. The old whaddayaknow…. There's a saying that one can never leave an evil place with live souls." His eyes are starting to drift again. I push his shoulder a little.

"Blue. Wake up, brother." He snaps to and shakes his head. "What'd you do, kill everybody in the place?" I say this just as a joke but when he looks at me I know that it isn't. He winks at me. Suddenly, I know what I have to do.

"Cin. Thanks, man."

"Sure, Blue," I say, understanding that I need to get just a small piece of whatever it is he has. "Anytime."

The car sunk when Blue got into the passenger side. "Whoooeeee! Here we go! You ready for this, Cin?" he said in a strange voice. His throat struggled with every syllable. I've never seen him like this. I don't know what the hell he's on. It can't just be testosterone. Guess I don't blame him though. Everybody needs to jump out of their skin once in a while.

"I sure hope I'm ready, Blue." I put the car into reverse

and back out of my parking spot. "Why don't you take me to the hospital."

"What? I'm not going back there. Why do you want to go there? Are you gonna turn me in?" He looks at me sideways. He knows I'd never do that, though.

"I need some painkillers, brother. And not the dopey kind you got," I say, ready to find the place whether he wants me to or not. I put the car into drive and we begin to cruise out of the lot, the lights they finally installed in the complex beating down on us, outlining our every scar through the windshield. The tiny knot shaped by a rock at some point opened up to it, sprinkling little extremes of light all over us.

"Well, they'll be looking for me. Now, maybe, you too. But you can just say you didn't know what was going on," Blue says. I scan the buildings, each holding it's own unit of creatures. They'd just painted, too, so it looked almost respectable in our quiet little jungle. I know though, that when it's daylight, if I look really close, I can see the ugly, the terrified, through a slice of a broken blind here or a dirty curtain fallen open there.

We pulled into the lot after cruising by it a couple of times to make sure the cops hadn't come yet. It was still the night shift. No one will discover the bodies for another hour or so, when the day shift rolls in. The building is very still, a light winking in one of the bigger windows. I look over at Blue and his head has fallen back on the head rest. His eyes are only half open but I know he sees everything. He doesn't say anything when I open the car door to go in, through the first floor window he'd climbed out of. He wanted to stay in the car. I drew a mental map of the place when he explained it to me. It was simple considering the window I'd be climbing through brought me right into the medicine lab and his room was just down the hall from there. I look in the window, having to stand on my toes and, before anything else, I smell what must be death. I throw up right away, on the grass, right outside the window; then I pull myself up

42

through the mouth of it. I'm careful not to slip in the blood that has come from the guy's throat. So much blood and one little throat. Jesus. I grab whatever pill bottles I can from the cabinet and stuff them in Blue's backpack, which I'd emptied before I left the car. I look around. The razor is sitting in the guy's blood, I can barely see its outline there by his arm. I hold my breath and pick it up. I wash it in the sink beneath the cabinet, use some soap. I dry it on my pants. I press my thumb and first finger onto the dull end. I lick it. I pull out a piece of my hair and stick it on its surface. I throw it back into the puddle where I found it and watch it drown in the red.

       I find the door to Blue's old room easily since it's the only one that was open. Some lady's got her head covered with a shirt and there's blood all over the floor and the front of her uniform. Her hand is clean so I kneel to pick it up with my own to study it for a minute, touching the ring there, her fingernails. I pull another hair from my head and weave it between her middle finger and first finger as best I can. I stand up and step over her. I sit on Blue's pillow, put my ass on his pillow. There is a little bear on the floor so I pick it up, lick his little plastic eyes and push my thumbprints into them before I put it under the nurse's arm. I walk back down the hall to the lab, step over the man and hop through the window.

       Blue is sitting in the same position when I get back into the car. We don't look at each other. I quickly drive out of the lot and get to the highway. The day crew will show up any minute. I drive and drive, south, both of us tense and silent until we hit the Oregon border.

IV

       "I can see why Devon chose Florida. Self-indulgent motherfucker. All that sun. Probably thought he needed a vacation after all his hard work," I say, trying to open Blue up. He's barely said a word all day. Finally he looks over at me and

43

then looks back towards the road.

"Yeah. And he's probably indulging in Angel right now. She's there by now. Can't believe she went to him after all this." His voice pops and I can tell he's trying not to cry. Don't know what to say, though, never know what to say to make somebody feel better.

"Hey. Do you know about any of these pills I got from the hospital? I want a really good muscle relaxer that won't put me to sleep. I need to keep driving, you know? But my head hurts. I need something." I push the backpack over to him. He begins pulling the bottles out, one by one.

"Here's one. This one'll make you feel nice. Not strong enough for me but good for the average-sanity Joe, if you know what I mean." He opens the container and taps a couple into his hand. He opens a bottle of water. "You don't even have to pull over. Here," he says, handing me the goods. He watches me while I chew and swallow the pills and then searches through his own stash for a little something for himself.

"Why does your head hurt?" he asks me. I take my time to answer, thinking.

"Too much fucking, too little sleep," I say, knowing he can't believe me. He knows I've always had trouble getting pussy. He looks over at me but I keep my eyes on the road.

"I know what you mean, man," he says, and then pauses for a second. "Well. Used to know what you mean, if you know what I mean." He laughs but it's an awkward sound. I don't join in. I feel him look at me. He stops laughing.

"Naw. We're probably in the same boat, to be honest," I say. We're quiet for a while.

I keep my eyes on the road and start to feel nice. It starts in my legs. I concentrate to make sure it's not going to screw up my driving. "Blue, though, I bet we could pull over into any stupid little dive and you could still get a nice piece of ass. You gained your weight back. You're still Blue." A ball-less Blue.

A Body is a Body

Oh, the things unsaid. Those are the loudest. I look over at him and he's smiling like he appreciated it. "Want to pull over?" I ask him.

"Naw. I don't care about any of that."

"Don't care about a nice piece of ass?" I look at him, not believing. I've seen too much to believe.

"Naw. I could always get it but I never really cared about getting it," he says.

"How could you not care about pussy? A man lives and dies for a nice piece of pussy. Least I do." I swallowed hard, thinking of the truth in that.

"Well, my dick doesn't mind a good piece but that's the problem. Don't have control over my dick, wish I did but I don't. People take advantage of that."

"It'd be nice if all the chicks took advantage of my dick…. That's something a man shouldn't complain about. Mr. Fucking Privileged."

"Ah, but it's not as nice as you might think. Not when you're a kid," Blue says. We're both sort of surprised that he actually said it, I think. People know about Blue but nobody, not even Blue himself, has ever really said anything about it. It's all too big.

We get through Idaho, then Utah with her rock forms that look like big mounds of God-shit, as Blue described them. I informed him that God doesn't shit. He asked where I came from, then. Never mind that. Colorado, North-Eastern corner of New Mexico, then Texas, which takes a long, hot ass time to get through. It's like in the movies with all the cacti.

We stop in this small-town diner there and everyone looks at us when we walk in, even though it's crowded. People even stop chewing until we sit down. I feel a little edgy but Blue, on his special meds, seems to laugh at it all. It's like in those old Westerns, Blue being the guy who isn't afraid of anybody but himself. I won't be surprised if someone starts twirling a gun.

"This is surreal," I say, sitting straight-backed.

"Isn't it? Hee hee." Blue leans back and spreads his arms out against the back of the booth-bench. His wrists are still bandaged and I can see tiny lines of blood where it soaked through. The whole place can see. It's almost like he's bragging.

"How could you not wanna live to see more of this kind of shit?" It's hard to take my eyes away from his bandages, they make me so mad. Then he suddenly seems to realize himself and takes them down. Puts them in his lap. He's about to say something and then doesn't. The waitress comes before he gets a chance to answer the question.

"I want a meat plate. You have some kind of meat plate?" Blue looks the lady in the face but she turns away immediately, starts looking at her order pad. She nods and takes the rest of our order. Before she turns away she looks towards the area where Blue's wrists are resting, curious. He raises them, then, and sets them, palms up, on the table in front of him. The waitress looks at his face and then turns away quickly. She returns with a huge steak knife and some forks. He looks at me and laughs. I just stare at him, hating. We hold each other's eyes for a while. Seems like hours. And he looks away first. Suddenly I realize there's something in me that he's terrified of.

I'm still watching Blue when a huge guy comes up to our table, saying, "I'm afraid we ain't got no meat left. You're gonna have to go down the street." His voice is loud but it doesn't need to be because the whole place has become quiet again. I feel at least forty sets of eyes on us. Blue turns his head slowly towards the man. His eyes move over his large body. He's quiet for a moment, thinking.

"Have you done gone and eaten it all, sir?" Blue asks calmly. My heart races. This is bad.

"What did you say, boy? You wanna run that by me again?" the man says to Blue, moving closer. Blue slides over on the bench and stands up. Blue's about the same height as the man but a third of the width. He moves close to the man's face.

"I was wondering, Jimbo," he says, touching the name tag on the man's shirt, "if you had been the greedy boy who'd perhaps gone and eaten the whole stash yourself. It certainly looks possible." The last word had come with a mouthful of spit, on purpose, I'm sure.

Jimbo jumps on Blue and they begin wrestling and punching each other. I see other men begin to stand. They inch over. Afraid as I've ever been, I grab the steak knife and get between Blue and Jimbo and the group of men coming closer. I swing at the group, making large arcs with my arm.

"Stay the fuck back! I'll cut you motherfuckers! Just stay the fuck away!" They stop but don't sit back down. I look behind me to check on Blue and see that Jimbo is on top of him with his hands around his throat. Blue's turning color, scratching at the man's face. I look back towards the other men and step back, closer to Blue. Then, in one smooth movement, I turn and push the knife into Jimbo's shoulder. The knife must be sharp. It entered his body as if it belonged there. I pull it out and bring it down again, punching it into him. He falls off of Blue and begins squirming around on his back. I let go of the knife and stand, bigger than ever. Blue sits up, coughing. I pull him to his feet and whisper into his ear:

"We've got to switch cars, brother."

A few miles away we found a used car lot that was under construction. It had a row of clunkers out back. No one would be looking for these plates for awhile. We have to keep moving. I'm so tired, though. Blue's gonna have to take the wheel while I....

V

"Am I gonna be OK?" I asked Dr. Sunshine, watching him close. I didn't want him hiding things from me. I'd been sitting across from him at his desk and he'd pushed all his

47

paperwork and instruments to the side so there was nothing between us.

"Well, Jimmy. We're going to have to do a CT scan on you. It's an X-ray machine that shows us your brain. You have several symptoms that indicate you may have something similar to a brain tumor." He looked at me, serious as I'd ever seen him. His hands were folded on the desk in front of him and suddenly I couldn't really feel anything. Suddenly I was standing next to him, outside of myself, trying to punch him in the fucking head.

"The seizures, the temporary paralysis, the vomiting. What you told me about the unusual sexual urges. These things occurring with such frequency tell me we need to look deeper into this. I can't just prescribe you something. I'm sorry, Jimmy," he said, finally looking away. The asshole pitied me. That's when I really realized this shit might be serious.

"Oh. Is that right?" I said, getting up to leave his office. Then I tripped over my own foot. He jumped up to help me off the floor but I hit his hand away.

"I'm sorry, Jim. I'm truly sorry. I have many things I can offer you for the headaches."

I'm angry. I should've got some more chances. When I think about this really hard I get pissed and test myself or God or whoever. I think about how I could do something good to make it go away, help someone. Or maybe I can die quicker, I think, like the more I sin, the less time I have and who cares. Maybe I can make it grow faster. Either way, I'm in control here. I can make the thing go away or I can make the thing grow. And that's all.

Chapter Four: Angel

A Body is a Body

I

I'm leaving Devon. When he didn't want me it was more interesting, when I had something to conquer. I'm an angel like that. He knows that. I put all my stuff, plus some cash from the stash I found under his mattress, in the backpack I came with. I take his bike, his better one, and start riding to the little motel a couple miles away. I'd heard it's cheap so maybe I can hang out a few days while I make a plan. Guess I can go anywhere now. Don't think I'll stay here in Fort Walton Beach even though long stretches of beach spoon the Gulf of Mexico, even though the wind pushes itself through my hair and I can feel little sparks of sand tapping my ankles as I pedal. It's so empty here. I could go run around naked if I wanted, just me and the Gulf and the baby jellyfish that look like little bells, too innocent, still, to sting. But I need the violence of human contact.

II

The dude at the front desk needs a fork through the jaw.

"Do I have a hole in my shirt or something?" I say. He looks up at me surprised like maybe he thought I couldn't talk.

"Um. No. I don't think so. Uh. Sorry. Can I get something for you, Ma'am?"

"Yeah, how about you get yourself a life, or a piece of cunt or whatever will make you quit staring at my tits. It's rude."

"Sorry...um...sorry." He looks down at his hands and starts picking at his fingernails like if he worked at it hard enough this was gonna solve the problem of his life.

"I want to stay for a week. How much for a week?" He stands there quiet, still looking at his fingers. "How much, dude? What's the problem? Your mouth doesn't work now?"

"Um...here's the menu...." He says, sliding over a raggedy brochure. I look it over. He peeks up at me, trying hard not to look at my tits or anything other than my face. I take some money out of my wallet and put it on the counter.

Angel

"Are you the boss here or what?"

"The boss is out of town for the summer," he says, looking up at me again, like to see what I think of that. "So…I'm pretty much the boss until September." He looks down at his hands again.

III

I get to the motel room and the quiet sings to me. It feels good to be alone, to be in a place where nobody I know can find me. My first time. I feel like a virgin.

I pull up my skirt and put my hand in my panties. I'm a virgin, a virgin with her dunes, her sand stretch, her gulf. And suddenly, I'm hit by a wave, a huge wave made of clouds and glory. Inside it, I die. I die. I die.

Chapter Five:
Cinnamon Jim

A Body is a Body

I

"What do you think happens when you die, Blue?" I'd asked him, looking back and forth between the shadows in his face and the darkening road in front of me. The sun was setting. He looked over at me and laughed like he knew what I was getting at, like I was digging into him about his suicide.

"Shut up, Cin. Your point has been noted. Let it go."

"No, I'm just wondering what you think, yo. Do you just lie there, you think there's a heaven? Like, what's gonna happen if you do kill yourself, what're you thinking about that second before you cut your wrists? You've done it enough times, I'm sure you got some ideas." Blue was quiet for a long time.

"I guess I'm thinking that I want it to stop. All of it. I want my memories to be tiny and insignificant. I want silence, you know, quiet. I don't think about where I'm going, only that I'm escaping into a place where it doesn't hurt anymore. It's like I'm a wound, see, and in my death I'll find the perfect pain reliever. There's nothing more to feel after it's all over," he said. I glanced over at him and saw that he was looking down at the scars on his wrists, touching them gently, like he was in love. I pulled over next to a sand dune. He looked at me like I was going to do something to him. I smiled.

"We're in Fort Walton Beach, Florida" I said, "we passed the sign a while back, yo. I hope Angel's mom was right about their location." I looked straight ahead at the empty road. I sensed him tense up. "We don't got money for a room so I'd say we should stay on the beach tonight and figure out exactly what we're gonna do in the morning. Those two lovebirds can't hide for long in a teeny town like this. Just look in all the local bars for those suckers." Blue didn't say anything so I just opened the car door and got out. He followed. Then there was quiet all around us. The ocean and silence. "Doesn't look so bad to me," I said, watching as the sun stooped to take a sip from the Gulf.

II

Cinnamon Jim

I popped a couple pain relievers and leaned back on my elbows to keep an eye on the sunset. Blue didn't touch his stash but watched his backpack like it was going to have a conversation with him and he was just waiting for it to say the first words. Finally he looked over at me.

"What do you think happens when you die?" he asked, beginning to run his fingers through the sand. I got a lump in my throat that came from somewhere I don't understand completely. I swallowed it down and held my breath for a second to keep it down.

"I think maybe that you go into a kind of dream state. Like when you die, you go to sleep and everything you think is real is made up of symbols and shit that stand for whatever life you lived. I think death is a dream. You don't really die, your body dies and that's all," I said.

"Well that wouldn't do me much good, would it? My dreams seem to be one of the ugliest parts of my life."

"Naw. Guess it wouldn't." The sky was so beautiful then that it almost hurt. I didn't know what to do with it. I couldn't hold it; I couldn't put my tongue on it and taste it. Couldn't fuck it. I was wishing I could've taken it inside myself somehow, held it in my chest. The lump came back and I swallowed.

"I asked my mom once, when I was a kid, what happens after you die," I said.

"…What'd she say?" Blue asked after a while.

"She said that whatever a person believes will happen, will happen. But you really got to believe it, you know, you can't just say you believe it, I think. You can't just hope for it. There are those things you kind of hope for but then there're those things that you truly believe, deep down, you know?"

"Well, what would you hope for?"

"Heaven, of course. Whatever the hell that means. Maybe heaven means something different for everybody. My idea of heaven is probably a lot different than yours, don't you think?" Blue laughed into the air at that and the ocean seemed to take the sound into itself like it were thirsty for it. "Well, what would heaven be for you, you crazy bitch?" I asked him. I couldn't help but laugh too, imagining. Then he got silent and really started thinking about it, I could tell.

"Well, I'd want to be in a place where I'd be sure I was protected. Sometimes it's like everyone is out to trick me or hurt me," he said. I looked over at his slouching body and yawned. I'd been driving all day and was tired, finally. "And maybe there would be somebody that I could love and not be afraid, someone that would never leave me. After you're dead you can't die, right? So this person couldn't even die and leave me. They would always be there to love me and have me love them." He was taking up the sand in big handfuls and then letting it spill out from the side of his fist, over and over.

"Would the love include lots of pussy, though?" I asked him. He kind of laughed and shook his head like I was stupid. But he's the one sexing everything that wiggles. I watched him push through the sand. "Do you think you sometimes let people, or make people leave you, though? You push people over the edge and away from you," I said. "You test until a person can't stand you anymore." I didn't look at him then but I felt his look.

"Do I? It's possible. Maybe I'm just used to feeling left behind and it's easier for me to deal with it if I somehow make them leave me. It gives me a certain sense of control over the situation. Everyone's going to leave me anyway, at some point, so I push them to leave me sooner instead of later when it would hurt more. The longer you know someone, the more you understand each other and the more difficult it will be when they leave you," he said, dusting off his hands like he was through with the sand.

"Maybe." I took a big breath and watched the sliver of sun fall beneath the horizon, leaving the colors to die slowly on their own.

"What about you? What's your heaven?" he asked me. He lay back beside me and covered himself with his jacket.

"Hm. In my heaven, everything would be allowed and nobody would get pissed. We'd all have the same rules, see. There'd be beautiful women everywhere and for all eternity they'd have this weird but never-ending desire for me. In every eye I'd look into there'd be a total understanding of my soul but also an unembarrassed yearning for my dick. And then, of course, I'd need a hard-on that lasted until forever. That would be pretty cool." My eyes started getting tired so I closed them and kept going. "The main thing would be that everyone would understand themselves and each other. Sometimes I think we already got that but nobody wants to say it, like we love pretending, humans have fun tricking themselves into believing they don't understand because we get bored without the violence and the hate and the games." I opened my eyes and couldn't help but yawn again. It's contagious. Blue yawned after me. We were quiet for a minute. I wasn't quite finished, though. "Yeah. Maybe that heaven'd be boring. Maybe I'd want heaven to be just like life, with all the sadness and the sickness." My voice suddenly sounded stupid, like I was trying not to cry. But I didn't care. Blue didn't care either; he just kept looking at the sky, listening or thinking or whatever. I took a breath. "I don't think I'd be so into it if I actually had all that, anyway. I'd get bored if the chicks were always chasing me. I guess I could see what you mean, about what you said earlier. Maybe a lot of the hard-on comes with the chase."

"Maybe," Blue said, his voice sounding tired. It was dark then and I felt a breeze that was too light to keep me from sleeping. The pills made my body comfortable. Calm. I took my sweatshirt and put it over me after pushing the sand into a kind of pillow. I heard Blue's sleep in his breathing. He breathed in long through his nose and out hard through his mouth, almost like the world was a balloon and he was trying to blow it up.

      I know I deserve it. God gave me the trick of lust and I fell for it, am falling for being the fool. I was also given the tool of compassion and was too stupid to use it. I opened my eyes once more to see the sky, bleeding out then into a million tiny stars. It was just too goddam beautiful. I've always known what I have, what my morality is made up of, and when I decided to go against it I sinned. I know what I should've done, knew even while I was doing the opposite. See, it's when you know a thing as wrong and you still do it. If you don't see the wrong then you're home free, you're an innocent. If only I could just make myself believe. *The girl acted like she wanted it. Coming in there with her short skirt and tube top. And her little flirty giggle. When Blue came toward her she went to the stall, not the goddam door. Girl could've got away. But she didn't. Probably didn't even want to.* I earned what I got, I understand, no matter what Mama or anybody says. Young as she is, I think the little sis's the only one who understands it. Alexa. Not that I told her what I did but that she could sense it in me. This is what was meant to happen, this is fate. God knew. But it only looks like justice from behind.

Chapter Six: Angel

Angel

I pushed through the door into the place and all the desperate suckers followed me with their seedy eyes. They were lined up around the bar like a mob of vultures waiting for a deadie to spread-eagle for their feasting pleasure. I made sure not to look any of them in the face. They always take that as an invitation, like to look at a guy is to offer up your pussy on plate. I was there for a drink, not a dick, so I kept my head lowered as I made my way to the far end of the bar.

"You're Angel, right?" the bartender asked me. He looked me over as I made myself cozy on the bar stool, like he had the law in his pants. I gave him a look full of junk but he didn't notice. Too busy bugging at my tits.

"How'd you know? Do I look like an Angel? Give me a whiskey, straight," I said. The guy was watching me in the mirror behind the bar while he made my order. I didn't see him doing it but I could feel it. Like a billion tiny monster hands, grabbing.

"Couple guys came in here checking for someone who looks like you," he said, setting my drink in front of me. A healthy one.

"Oh yeah? Two? One of them was Devon?" Poor guy was missing me already, I figured. But then maybe he was just sour because I took his bike.

"Naw. Not the one you came in here with the other times. One of them said they was Sin. Red hair, freckles all over the place. Other one looked kind of fucked up. High on something. When they described you I knew exactly who they was talking about," he said, his eyes glancing down at my tits again. I shivered. Those guys weren't supposed to be in town.

"What'd they say?"

"Just said they was wondering if you were ever around here. Asked about that guy Devon, too. I told them you and him been coming around the last couple nights. You just missed them by ten minutes."

"You just told them my business like that?" I asked him.

59

A Body is a Body

"They didn't seem like a threat or nothing. Just like they was looking for some old friends." He looked at me and leaned on the bar. In my space. I could smell his breath.

"What'd you drink a bucket of piss for breakfast?"

"What?"

"I can smell your breath. You're caught," I said, smiling my best sweet falsie. I put money for my drink and a good tip in front of him, between us. He stood up straight and scooped the money up.

"Cheers." He put the money for the drink in the register and the rest in his tip cup. I sipped my drink and the moment I put it down two stools on each side of me, the only empty ones at the bar, were taken. Cin and Blue. I almost choked.

"Blue. Oh shit, what the fuck. Cin? What are you guys doing here?" Suddenly my heart was racing like it was guilty. They were both leaning towards me, watching my face. Then they looked at each other.

"Where's Devon?" Cin asked. His voice was hard and his face was trying to work itself into an expression that would make me feel nervous. But I know Cin too well. It only made him look silly. He suddenly realized this and as I watched him he looked away, towards the bartender, and ordered him and Blue a drink.

"Don't come up in my space and start demanding shit from me. I don't owe you anything. Neither of you," I said. I looked the both of them in the face so they knew I was serious. Cin kind of bobbed his head Blue only half-looked at me. He was high. His eyes were bloodshot and wandering all over the place. "What's wrong with you, Blue?"

"What?" His eyes stopped wandering and settled on me. The second they did, his face gave in. His lower lip got weak and I was sure he was gonna start crying right there.

"Don't start that shit. What is this? How'd you guys get here and what's your plan? I hope you guys don't think you came

60

down here to be heroes and shit cause I'm not trying to be saved. And I don't know where that bitch Devon is cause he's not my business anymore." My hands were shaking when I took a sip of whiskey. They both watched it until I set the drink down. They looked at each other.

"So you guys aren't together?" Blue asked like the hopeful dummy he always is. His hand was inching closer to mine on the bar and I watched it, daring him, until it stopped a couple inches away. I saw he still had his bandages on. Crazy guy. I wonder if he actually used the razor I sent. Or maybe his whole act is just a bid for pity after all.

"Why should you be concerned with that? Nothing's changed, Blue. And don't expect me to feel guilty because of what happened between you and him. That's not my business either so don't start getting all weepy on my shoulder and acting like I'm responsible in some way. I'm not. You too, Cin, don't be stupid." Nobody said anything. The bartender brought their drinks and I ordered another. The two of them sat looking down at the bar. After a few minutes of quiet I held up my new drink. "To the Jungle," I said, "to our old life in the Jungle. And our new lives somewhere else." They picked up their glasses and touched mine but neither of them looked at me.

"Where're you guys staying?" I asked, even though I knew the question might imply an invitation to my motel room and that idea disgusted me. They looked at each other, seeming to decide who was gonna answer the simple question.

"So far, in the car," Cin said finally, trying to keep the hope of an invitation out of his voice.

"How long you guys been sleeping in the car?"

"Probably four or five days," Blue said.

"That's why you smell like a couple of assholes. You have money?"

"Most of it went to gas to get here. You know the old cars are bad on gas," Cin said.

"Well. Shit. I guess you guys can come stay at the motel with me. But don't think you're gonna stay for a century cause I need my space. You get your showers and figure out what you're doing and then you exit like the good little punks you are, yeah?"

"Yeah. Of course. Thanks."

"Yeah, thanks, Angel," Blue says. I looked at Blue and knew what he was thinking.

"And you guys are sleeping on the floor. I don't give a shit if there're bugs. I'll ask the motel guy for some blankets. You guys aren't staying in the bed with me and I want you to fucking understand that." They looked at each other and nodded at me, as they've always done. We settled with the bartender who'd obviously been all in our business since the second they walked in. Devon's gonna know.

Chapter Seven: Blue

A Body is a Body

I

I peer through the blinds and look for my Angel- look, without truly wanting to see. I'm almost certain she is fooling with the motel office boy. She has been too long in the office, hours it seems, and now Cin has begun to chew at my psyche. I turn my back on the window and face him. The sun has spoken and a million spots have formed in protest on his cheeks, his forehead. His upper lip is sweating; my ability to see this makes me realize he's too close to my face. I step to the side but his gaze is relentless, asking me for things, asking me to respond to what he's saying. I turn away and shuffle through my backpack to find my pills. I pop them. One. Two. Three.

"You only know how to be a victim, Blue. That's all you ever are and it's boring. It's selfish," he says, his cheeks wallowing on every syllable. At the tail of each sentence he throws out his hand to accentuate his point. It's almost as if he's dancing. He is squinting at me through the rays of sunlight that have speared their way through the slits in the blind. His voice is attacking the air between us like a hatchet. I watch his lips moving and feel a little sick. They seem so obscene, chapped and peeling from the sun. Then he says nothing for a few minutes, waiting for me to reply. I don't say anything, can't really make myself say anything. I move to pull a swatch in the blind again to see if Angel's on her way from the office. She's not. I suspect she might be fucking the office boy or preparing to fuck the office boy. Cin looks at me as I watch for her. "How could anybody fall for somebody who's too weak to hold himself up? And you're always like this. There are no good times for you, yo. You're always crying and moping around," he says. He turns to sit in the chair and I go back to my place on the bed. I get up again to look through the blinds. I think I see some movement in the office window. Only for a moment though. Only a flash. Maybe they went to his room. "You're weak. You're weak and it's corny. You think you shouldn't have to deal with the world.

Everybody has to, though. When're you going to step outside of yourself, out of your small little sad head, and see that?" I let the blinds snap shut and look at Cin.

"I deal with life, I just have a different way of dealing with it. I sift through it with a different brain, different fingertips," I say to him, full of calm.

He's probably got her in his room and is fucking her in the ass, the office boy. She loves it in the ass. She told me once that getting fucked in the ass is a moving experience, that pain is very much part of the pleasure and that there is a sort of hyper-intimacy between two people aware of this dichotomy.

"Pain is very eloquent," I say.

"Oh, bullshit, yo. You just want to make it like your pain is something extra special. Everybody feels shitty sometimes, though, everybody gets fucked every now and again. But you talk the big talk to make your pain seem higher than all other pain so you got an excuse for your constant moping. Even before Devon did what he did. You're always like this." He's breathing hard and his eyes have started to sparkle. "Sure, you were hurt. Bad. Nobody's denying that. But it almost seems to me like you wanted it, like maybe it gave you more ammo to fuck the people around you with. Now you got their pity for life, right? You're the goddam king of victims now, yo. Your pain can't be questioned anymore so it's cool if you suck all the good feelings out of everyone. You take everything possible. From everybody that lets you, you take." I look at him and lie back on the bed, stretching my arms out on both sides and crossing my feet. I feel the medicine begin to work.

"They give because they want to, Cin," I explain. "And in exchange for what people give me, for what you say I take, I make them feel. Everyone implies happiness is all there is to live for but it's no kinder than sadness, than misery. Once one feels happy, there's nothing more to reach for. Happiness becomes a sort of end, a death of hope, of yearning, of feelings. Happiness breeds monotony and boredom. And these are the biggest evils to a soul. Everyone knows this. It is why people like you, Cin, find yourselves drawn to people like me. It can be more potent than happiness. It's heavier. Sadness is more real. See? You can feel it; you can taste it in me. I am pure with it." I close my eyes, making the world black, while I feel myself dieing a little every moment that Angel isn't in the room. She's fucking the office boy, fragmenting her womanhood with the repetitive giving of herself. Always giving. "Pure. See, happy people always have a little of me lurking behind the eyes. They are never fully happy, like I am wholly unhappy. There's no such thing as complete happiness. They're frauds, the happy people. They act as though they don't want anything but to be happy but they do, Cin, you do. I'm only honest about it, I don't pretend. I am truth; misery is truth. It's all that's real." I open my eyes and look towards him. He's watching me with pity and a strange longing. Then he seems to tense up and it's as if he's not looking at me anymore but the air between us. He falls and begins shivering. I get up quickly and kneel down beside him, try to hold up his head. Some kind of convulsion. But it's over in a few seconds. When he comes to he seems both surprised and irritated. I ask if he's alright and finally he focuses on me.

"Yeah. I'm cool. You can let me go. It was just a seizure. Everything's cool. I just need to relax for a second." I get up and sit on the bed, feeling my body warm.

"You took too many pills," I tell him, hoping this doesn't interrupt my high. He shakes his head yes and gets up to get a glass of water. I feel myself melting so I lay back. I smile and relax and nod. Then Angel comes through the door.

II

She has come, as she has every day since they found me after Devon left with my treasures. She has dressed my wound. We're both silent now and have been silent since she walked

*through the door. I touch her nose, her lips, and she lets me. I lay
there and watch her but I want to rise up and step inside her; so
quiet now, and sweet, full of truth. A truth she tries to hide. But
just for a moment I want to feel that special truth as my own. To
kiss her, even to make love to her is not enough; there is still a
barrier of skin and body that keeps me from wholly touching her.
I stand up and look at her and she looks up at me with eyes that
see me and love me still. There is pity there, but it is a confused
pity, one that, perhaps, she hadn't realized existed. Hadn't
wanted to believe existed. Now she looks at my stomach, my
chest, my chin, my forehead. She won't look in my eyes. Then
she looks down, almost embarrassed, as if she shouldn't have
been looking.*

*"Angel?" I say. I want to cry for her, her pity. She looks
at me then, into me, through my eyes. But only for a moment. I
fail and grow strong with that look; am weak but proud. I feel
she loves me. She feels me. And like that part of herself that she
tries to hide, that she pretends she doesn't want, she needs me too
to hide, to disappear so she can grow rich in her masked life.
Her life full of wilted joy. A façade will not help her. She will
see. Agony and truth live in the very bones.*

"Blue! What the fuck is wrong with you? Wake the fuck
up. Get him some water Cin. His eyes are finally open." Angel's
face is hovering above me, the light from the lamp making her
stray hairs glow with translucency. I instinctively reach up to
bring her face closer to mine. "What the fuck are you doing,
man?" she says, jerking away, "are you asking to be punched in
the chest? Quit that shit." Cin comes over with some water.

"Always taking care of you, aren't we Blue?" He holds
my head up to help me drink.

"Fuck you," I say, looking him in the eye. "Don't help me
if you're going to complain about it. I don't need help. Unless
you want to pass me my backpack there."

A Body is a Body

"Crackhead," says Cin, tossing the bag onto my very queasy stomach. I gag and Angel cusses Cin for almost causing me to vomit on her pillows.

"And you quit your giggling, Blue. As if you threw up on my pillows and it would be Cin's goddamn fault. You're the one who can't handle your shit." She looks at me for a second then looks over at Cin, resting her fists on her hips. "So. When are you guys going to get the hell out of here?" Cin and I look at each other. Then I lay back. Just for a moment:

To herself she is only a small thing; a woman, a heart. But I can see how she is something else, too. Angel is the only person I've ever seen with a river. She's got a rush of violence, of sex, of love running through her like a river. She is not aware of this but if she were, she wouldn't know what to do with her hands, how to hold her head, the particular angle at which she should smile at another being. Having a river is a terrifying responsibility. One must know how to feed the fish and carry the rafts. And just now her river leaks again, from the pink inner corners of her eyelids. She looks up at me, her brown eyes seeming bigger and more vulnerable than ever. They drift down to my chest, then dart back up to my eyes again to see, maybe, if it's alright with me, her looking. Does she want to fuck me? But my bandages.... I look down at my body and realize my jeans hang low and the line of hair that creeps downwards from my stomach meets the patch of pubic hair above the top seam of my jeans. This is what people want. I look at her eyes looking and, for a second, I find her grotesque. She is like the others.

"You gonna tell us where Devon lives?" I hear Cin ask carefully. I look up to see his eyes fluttering between Angel and me. Angel stares at him, quiet for a minute.

"I don't want to get into that shit. You guys want to mess him up, you do it on your own. He's probably already fucked up anyway, alone like he is."

"You talk like you forget what he did to me," I say,

watching her eyes. She doesn't look at me but starts examining her fingernails, probably dirty with sand from the beach earlier. Or the skin from the office boy's back.

"None of that's my business. That's between you and him. And Cin, if he decides he wants to be a part of that craziness," she says. I look over at Cin. His face is turned away from me as well, studying the lampshade.

"What're we gonna do to him anyway?" Cin asks, still playing with the lamp. I suddenly realize that the revenge gnawing at the edges of my soul means nothing to them. Justice is nil. I also understand that it is simple to obtain a razor blade from any drugstore and that to die here in the warm sand, the blood streaming from my body and into the Gulf would be as natural and beautiful as the earth itself. But this doesn't sound so delicious as it did two days ago. Cin turns on the lamp and eyes the shade with interest. He turns it off. Angel has split the blinds and stands near the window now, shredding the light and shadows of the room with the pressure of her fingertip. Her lips move in thought. Cin begins flicking the lamp off and on, on and off, staring at it as if it might answer his question. Then Angel releases the blind. One hand fools with the thumbnail of the other and she doesn't look up for a while but keeps her eyes locked on her hands, lightened and then darkened by the potent lamplight. A rush moves in a wave over my body. Maybe there is another way to solve this.

"Maybe I could just ask him why. Talk to him." I feel alone in the room. Their silence, two-minutes heavy, leaves me to myself. I braid my fingers together. Unbraid them. Then I sit up and swing my legs over the side of the bed. They look at me.

"Talk?" they say, together, looking at each other with doubt.

"Yes. I always look for revenge. That hasn't brought me so far though, has it?" I look at them both, wondering if they'll believe me. Wondering if I believe myself. They have both stopped with their fidgeting, their avoidance of the conversation we're having.

"You serious, brother?" Cin asks. I nod my head. Angel looks at me furtively, from the corner of her eye; from where this all started.

III

I'm walking home across the lot from the mall where I was looking for a purple shirt for Angel. She looks beautiful in purple. I've never spent this much time with anybody except my mother. It's our anniversary today and I can't wait to get home to her. She'll love it. I wonder if she got me anything. Good. The light's still on, she's here. The door is locked, though, why is the door locked?

I can hear them the second I get it open. I know exactly who it is. I can smell their sex from the kitchen. I can hear them. I'll kill him. He knows. There's a knife lying in the sink, sure as a prophecy, so I grab it and kick the bedroom door in.

"Shit! What the fuck are you doing home this early, Blue? You said you'd be a couple hours!"

"It's been three hours, Angel."

"Whoowee. Three hours! Who's the man!" Devon beats on his chest like an ape. I look him in the eye and as soon as I do his eyes drop down to my hand holding the knife. Angel looks there too. They get really quiet, look towards each other for a second. A few moments huff by as I'm trying to decide how I'll go about this.

"What's that knife for? Blue. Give it to me."

"Are you making a joke, Angel baby?" They've both got up to stand and I look at them, sweaty and pathetic, afraid like animals caught in a corner. Devon's dick's fallen soft and his face shows that he's trying to find an exit. His chest pumps back and forth. He knows what I'm going to do. It takes three strides to reach him and I swing the knife, getting him deep in the arm.

70

Blue

"Fuck, Blue! I'm sorry, man. I'll make it up to you. Just let me go. Shit! Look at my arm, man. I'm gonna bleed to death!" He's dripping all over the sheets and comforter. I watch it seep out.

"How long do you think that might take?" I ask, moving towards him again.

"C'mon, man! We grew up together. Not over a bitch, Blue, not over this bitch." I feel calm and sure. He is so naked, vulnerable. It won't take much. Somehow, though, he jumps over the bed and shoots out the door. Almost as soon as he disappears I don't care about him because now Angel and I are facing each other. "Angel? Angel, Baby. What's going on?"

"Blue, you went too far just now!"

"What? Baby, he was trying to have sex with you."

"And I wanted him to. I asked him to." Her eyes look hard and serious when she says this. Her nostrils flare. I am trying to figure out what she means but it just doesn't make any sense. Her breasts, the color of falling autumn, blush and move as she breathes. It's like she can't suck in enough air. She sees me looking and grabs the sheet to cover herself. "It's over, Blue. It's been over."

"Just all of a sudden like this?"

"You know it's not all of a sudden. Stop being stupid. I've been telling you and you just pretend like you don't understand. Like now. No more, Blue. I'm tired. No more soap opera bullshit."

"But in my bed, Angel?" She looks down, ashamed at first, I think. Then she lifts her face slowly and there is a strange smile there.

"I'm sorry about that. I didn't expect it to happen like this," she says. I have to turn my head and vomit. She jumps back. I look at her and wipe my mouth. Bringing up the knife, I approach her. Suddenly, she opens her lips and laughs louder than I've ever heard her.

A Body is a Body

IV

I come to, needing water terribly. I grab the glass on the table next to the bed and spill it all over my chest. When I move to get up my head pulls me back down to the pillow, heavy as a heartbreak. Angel floats through my mind like a balloon I've accidentally released into the air. Every pore in my body wants it back.

Chapter Eight: Angel

Blue's nodding again. Crackhead. I'm flicking through the channels, waiting for something to catch me when Cin starts jerking around next to me. We're sitting on the floor at the end of the bed so he doesn't fall too hard. But his head hits first. He must've taken too many pills.

"Cin! What's wrong with you?" I say. I get up to get some water to throw on him. But then he stops. He looks around, like stunned. I give him the water and when he puts it to his mouth I see blood there.

"Bit my tongue," he says, wiping it with his thumb and looking at it.

"What just happened there, man? You freaked me out." He takes his time answering me like what just happened didn't. I ask him again.

"I just had a seizure. It's done. Don't worry about it."

"What do you mean don't worry about it? You just had convulsions on the floor. What's wrong with you? You taking too many pills?" He won't even look at me. Cin is hiding something. He puffs out his cheeks, rinsing his mouth. Bet that tastes nasty. Blood. "You never had seizures before. Why are you having seizures?" He still doesn't say anything. I watch him sip his water. His hand is bony and it looks like his face is sucking into itself as I watch it. "And why are you so skinny? Why don't you want to eat?" He looks at me like he wants to say something but he can't. I feel my heart, suddenly. "What's happening to you, Cin?" I feel scared and like I don't want to know the answer. For a while we just watch each other and as we do it seems like the blood is draining out of me. My fingers feel cold. I'm sweating. Then he raises his glass, presses his eye to it, like looking at me from below the water line there. His eye is magnified. I don't want to look at him anymore but then I can't look away, either. He's quiet for a long time.

"I'm dieing, Angel. I'm dieing and it hurts," he says finally, his voice very small. It's like I knew he was gonna say that. I don't feel surprised. I don't know what I feel. Maybe like I'm gonna float up and hit my head on the ceiling.

"Where does it hurt?" I say, barely able to hear my own voice. He puts the glass down and touches his forehead with five skinny fingertips. His eyes are watering now. And I feel my own doing the same. "Why didn't you tell me before?" I say, about to cry for real now. I can't help it. It's coming up my throat like a swarm of bees.

"I thought maybe I could make it go away. I thought I wouldn't have to tell anybody."

"Make it go away?" I ask, moving towards him. I put my arms around his neck and lay my head on his shoulder. I don't want to look at his eyes anymore. They're too big. Or too old.

"Yeah, see, I have this thing with God. I think if I do some good things to make up for all the dirty shit I've done then the thing will go away. I won't die. It's only a matter of balance, Angel," he says, leaning his head on mine.

"What is it?"

"A tumor. In the front part of my brain."

"Can't they just cut it out?" I say, thinking I should've used better words. I squeeze him.

"Not one like this," he says, taking my hand and squeezing it. He doesn't let it go. I want to run. I wanna pretend I never heard any of this. But then I want to kiss him, too. I want to make him forget. So I do. I turn and kiss his head. Once, twice, three times. Then I kiss his eyes. They're wet. I take his hands and close my eyes. I kiss his chin, his nose. His mouth.

Chapter Nine: Devon

A Body is a Body

"Can I have a vodka cranberry on the rocks, please," I say to the bartender who's checking his hair in the mirror. He turns around and starts making the drink.

"Bet you're having a hard week," he says, setting my drink in front of me. I just look at him, waiting for him to add something to his information about my business. "Them two guys coming in here to snatch up your girl." The guy laughs and I can see little crumbs in his mustache. I just watch him and sip my drink. I look over his build and see that I could take him. I look into his face and he seems to also realize this. "Aw. Don't worry over a bitch like that. She tosses her pussy around like junk mail, sends her shit out to whoever'll open her." I can't help but laugh a little at this and the guy seems glad enough to see me smile. "Listen. Next one's on the house," he says, winking. He turns to one of the locals who nods for another round.

On the way here I saw them. And Cin saw me. I biked past a driveway and saw them standing there talking, Blue facing the opposite direction, gesturing and saying something, Cin facing me. And he saw me. His eyes followed mine, dipping back and forth between me and Blue, for probably 20 seconds before I made it beyond his sight. I pedaled faster thinking they would come after me but nothing happened. They didn't follow. Or maybe they are following and'll be here any minute. I take another long drink until the glass is empty, then catch the bartender's eye for another. He makes it and sets it in front of me. "Like I said. On the house."

I'm on my fourth drink when Blue and Cin walk in. I feel high and ready. Cin sees me almost immediately and pulls Blue over to a table as far away from the bar where I'm sitting as possible. They sit down and Cin looks down as Blue's eyes make their way over to me. I'm tense but when he looks at me finally my stomach drops. I took his balls. I finish my drink. There's no apologizing. There's not a thing in the world I can do to convince him not to tear out my heart. My palms are sweating when I look to the bartender for another drink, not because I want one but because I don't know what the fuck else to do. His testicles are in my closet and I realize suddenly that I might be a little crazy. No. What he did to Jenna. It fits, it all makes sense. I had a right. I am right. I can feel his eyes though, and they're cutting into my back like I was wrong. I drink. No, whatever he does to me is fair. I know.

I call the bartender over and have him send some whiskey shots over to their table. I tell him as many as they want. I tell him to charge everything to me. I tell him give me a shot too. I swivel around in my stool when all the shots have been delivered and raise my drink to them. They look at me then look at each other. They raise their glasses. I order some more shots. The more I drink the less it will hurt. Third round and they're whispering to each other like to decide what to do. I go to them, hitting a table corner on the way. Hardly felt it. Tomorrow I will. They're both watching me as I pull a chair up to the table. We just sit there for a good minute without saying anything. I understand now, I understand, "I understand," I say, my voice full of stupid, of drink. I look right at Blue's eyes, finally, and feel something like pity inside, I guess, like maybe he should never have met a monster like me. Suddenly he reaches his arm across the table and hits me. It's quick and it feels more surprising than painful. I'm stunned for a second. I look at Cin and his eyes are big and staring at my cheek. I look down at the table and there's blood, a lot of blood, spreading over it like somebody spilled their drink. And a piece of broken glass. OK. I'm hurt. He got me with glass. What else is he gonna do. Napkin. Face. I glance up at Blue and he looks confused like he doesn't understand what's going on. Cin looks over at the bartender and starts pushing at Blue. They get up and run out of the bar. My face aches. I can't stay awake.

Chapter Ten: **Blue**

A Body is a Body

I

"Blue's awake now, Cin. You got all your shit together?" Angel's standing there looking back and forth between me and Cin. She's holding a glass of water. She must've taken us in after we left Devon. "Here. But you gotta sit up and drink it yourself. I'm not your nurse." She pushes the water into my useless palm and I drop it, the wet darkening my lap. My hand is too weak right now. "Damn. Can't you even hold a little glass of water?... Here, here's another one." She puts a second glass on the bedside table. "Pick it up when you can handle yourself. But you guys gotta hurry. I don't want to be getting in trouble for your bullshit." I breathe and try to feel my body beneath the cloud of the morphine.

II

"What the fuck, Blue! I thought we were just gonna talk to him," says Cin. We're sitting between some sand dunes now, safe and warm. I look at Cin and don't know quite what to say. I don't know what happened either. There was the glass lying on the floor beside my chair and then it was in my hand and then Devon's face seemed to come into it like a child to its mother. "I... don't really know. It just happened."

"Fuck 'it just happened,' Blue, fuck that. Now we're gonna have the coppers up our ass."

"Oh, yes. The coppers. They will be coming for me." I open my pack and see I only have a few of the good pills left. I don't know how to get more and I'm afraid. Maybe I should go back to the place. "I have to go back," I say, watching Cin's bottom lip heave slightly with the coming and going of his breathing. I shake the pill bottle.

"Go where?... Uh uh, Blue. You can't go back there. You're fucked if you go back there. They're not gonna give you some more morphine and send you on your way, they're gonna kick your ass and throw you in a cage to get your pretty ass raped every night by the toughies, yo. Fuck that. You're not going back there. And neither am I. Not until I'm done."

"Done? With what? They're going to get me eventually anyway. Better I go now so I can get out sooner… and you know, I'm pretty good at taking it in the ass," I say, almost laughing to myself. "I think I can handle it. I just need them to hook me up, give me some pills." Cin is looking at me strangely but I don't care what he knows about me.

"Listen. We can find that shit on the street somewhere. You're not going back to that place right now. And Blue, they're never gonna get you for anything. Not if you shut the fuck up about it. Not if you straighten up first, let me do what I'm trying to do for you. " I lay back in the sand, waiting for him to explain. He only watches me for a moment, though, and then gets up and heads towards the shore, his figure cringing under the late afternoon sun.

My entire body is cringing inside, like it has many times in my life, only this time I can't move to at least make the experience slightly more tolerable. I don't understand what he is doing to me. My dick is numb. My balls are numb but there's some pulling there. Maybe he is sucking me. I hope he is only sucking me. But he has that tool, that sharp tool. He can't be sucking me, he is breathing too clearly, too heavily.

I open my eyes and look to see Cin throwing stones into the surf. The sun is beginning to fall behind where the water ends and I can't think of anything more beautiful. Even Cin, standing in the water with his pants rolled up, is something incredible, what's left of the sun crowning his head, sewing itself through his hair to make him look more like itself. (*"I'm taking all your hormones away here, I'm taking your children. No more loving for you."*)

I sometimes understand that love is just an idea, something the human mind has invented to protect itself from hopelessness. As I lie here watching Cin, I love him but I wonder if it is a love molded by hope. He gives me a certain hope that something other than my own pain exists, my own body. (*This isn't about Jenna. Jesus, what is he doing? I'm cold. And he kisses me. He loves me and is punishing me for it. But what is he doing? My eyes. I can open them. I can breathe.*)

Cin is digging in the sand now. He's taken off his shirt and the last drop of sunlight is pouring over his spine, which juts out from his skin now like thirty little daggers. He is sick.

What has he done? God. I want to die. I want to die. I want to die. It hurts, oh God it hurts. Everywhere. I feel it everywhere. Please. Make it stop. God. Think of something beautiful. Think of Mother. Think of her pretty, soft hair and touch it. God. There is nothing. He cut me there. Why did he cut me there? No. He cut me there. Please. I want to die. Please take me. I need somebody. I need help. But it hurts too much. I need help. I need help. I need

"help—" I breathe deep, like I just came from under water. Cin is standing over me, scrutinizing my face.

"Brother, what's up? What's wrong with you? Are you hurt?" I collect the pieces of myself that haven't been destroyed yet.

"Uh, yeah, I'm alright. Just fell asleep, you know? Bad dreams."

"Bad dreams, huh?" He looks down at me but I can't tell what the expression on his face looks like. It's shadowed. I feel almost like he's threatening me. "So what are you gonna do about that? Kill yourself?" He laughs. There's something changing in him. He's becoming some other kind of creature. I watch him and his small movements seem grotesque. Greedy. We're quiet for a minute. "Hey. I need a pill, man. Pick me out a pill." I reach for his bag and wonder why he hasn't learned which pills he should take yet, why he doesn't want to find them himself.

"How are we going to get some money? And what about

Angel?"

"What about her? She's not a part of this and doesn't want to be a part. You gotta forget about her for now." He's quiet while he moves to sit next to me. "She forgot about you a long time ago anyway, brother," he says, putting his hand on my shoulder and looking at me, "at least in that way." I shrug him off, burning inside, and reach to find his pills. "We can hit Devon's house for cash…. I finally got his address out of Angel," he says after a long pause. He downs the muscle relaxers. "I'm sure he's got a good stash going there. But I'm gonna go inside by myself. I don't want you having any more 'accidents' with sharp edges." I nod my head and look down. "Well. Let's get going. You OK?" He holds out his hand to help me up.

"OK as I'll ever be, I guess," I say, taking his hand and rising.

"Whatever, Blue." Cin starts walking ahead of me. His dark shape points over the water at the final colors of the day: "Just look at that. Just see that and decide what your life is." He walks a few more steps.

Then my oldest friend falls face-first into the sand.

Chapter Eleven:
Cinnamon Jim

A Body is a Body

"Listen. In a minute, I'm gonna drop back," I say, checking over my shoulder. "You just keep walking, Blue. Don't turn around, alright? Just keep walking, no matter what. Promise me. You gotta keep walking. Get in the car and drive." Blue looks at me, trying to understand. I look back. Movement. Someone is trying to hide back there. I'm suddenly cold but I shake it off.

"Who is it?" Blue asks me. He looks at me. He puts his hands in his pockets but keeps walking. I fall back a little.

"Ain't gonna help nothing if both of us go down. Remember that, alright? When they start asking you questions. Promise."

"Here we are," Blue says, searching my eyes for what I'm thinking. But even I don't know what I'm thinking. I just know my heart is racing and it's starting to get really warm outside. I lick sweat from my upper lip. It tastes sweet.

"Well, let's go," I say, pushing my arms through my pack. He puts on his pack and we start walking very slowly down the driveway towards the house.

"You don't have to come with me, you know." I say, looking over at him.

"I'm not going all the way. You don't have to freak out about that anymore," he tells me.

"I don't?" I say. Blue shakes his head no. I believe him.

He has stopped walking now and is looking at me strangely, his eyes squinting, his mouth hung open. I keep walking but slow, so he can hear me.

"Look, I'm not gonna worry about anything except that you just keep your pretty ass out of jail and in the world. You still got chances, Blue, you can still have a life if you really want it. But if you keep up like you've been doing you're not gonna have shit except for a sore asshole and a black eye." He laughs a little.

Cinnamon Jim

"And who's going to give me the black eye?"

"It's either gonna be me or your cellmate, Mr. Monster Cock." He gives me the finger and we start giggling like a couple schoolgirls. Then a woman in pink hot pants and a tube top comes walking up the drive toward us.

"Can I help you with something? You looking for a room, boys? I got a vacancy." She stops about ten steps in front of us and looks us over. Blue first, then me. When she reaches my eyes she stops, seeming to understand immediately. Then her eyes drift down to my dick. They hover there as it grows.

"Where are we?" Blue asks. I laugh a little inside.

"Don't worry, brother. I know exactly where we are," I say to him. He looks at me like he gets it, finally.

"I'm going to hang back, Cin."

"Good," I say to my friend. "Thank you." I turn to the woman. "Sure. I'll be needing a room. You got a nice suite for me?"

"Sure do, honey. But you're gonna have to share it with me and my friend, Pussy," she says. A second woman peaks at me from the doorway. "And don't worry. Since you have to share I won't charge you." She holds out her hand, smiling; I take it and press it to my lips.

Chapter Twelve: Blue

A Body is a Body

Alexa lays her head on my lap, now, and I run my hand over her hair. I feel her body jerk with a sob now and then. I know there's nothing much I can say to her. Nothing can unsqueeze the knot in her chest. Time, maybe. But time is never in a hurry when you're hurting. Never in enough of a hurry.

Cin's gone and he's taken my bad deeds with him. I tried to tell them all that I had done it, took the lives of those people, but no one listened. They said they had evidence that Cin did it. Fingerprints, hair. They also reminded me that I had been living in an asylum for the insane. They could see how I could get confused. Dr. Sunshine and my dear, dear Albert didn't say a word about why I was in there (however, they did publish a book resulting from a ten-year study on male castration).

But Alexa. She believes me. She knew Cin better than anyone in the world. Even himself.

Angel finally drifts into the room. Her face is tender with apology and she sits down next to Alexa and me. She rubs Alexa's back and kisses my face. Two hours pass before the three of us unwrap ourselves from each other and go out to soak up the air, breathe in the sunlight.

I spot him first. He's watching us from behind a tree across the street, hiding behind nature. I touch Angel and tell her, point him out to Alexa. They look up to see Devon, now acting as though he were never watching us but admiring the tree. I think I'm the only one with the idea but then I realize all three of us are waving him over. He looks at us as if he doesn't believe us, doesn't trust. But then he strolls over. No one says anything. By the time he sits down I believe we're all wondering if those are tears on his cheeks. After a moment though, we realize it is just a medicinal salve from where I sliced his face.

Chapter Thirteen: Angel

A Body is a Body

I bite my lip and shake the doctor's hand. I lay back on the table. She tells me to put my feet in the stirrups so I do, trying to keep my knees together. Of course she pushes them aside. But gentle. It's just me and her in here but it feels like the guys are here too. It's like I can feel their eyes.

Now a nurse is here, asking if I want to hold her hand. I tell her no. I tell her I want to do this by myself. The doctor pushes in a scapula. Not so cold because she warmed it in hot water. I hold my breath. Doctor tells me to breathe. I try not to look at the machine. They use clear tubes to suck, like to see what's coming out. Wonder if they could see an actual body part. No. It's only the size of my pinky nail, they said. She asks if I'm ready. I nod my head and she tries to smile, like to comfort me. They said it won't hurt. Maybe some cramping. I turn my head towards the wall and let some tears out. I think about how the soul of this one must carry on to the next. I think about how the soul must wait.

The nurse moves to turn on the machine.

"Wait," I say. "Wait."